MON

TAKING FLIGHT

TAKING FLIGHT

•

Connie Cox

AVALON BOOKS
NEW YORK

Published by Thomas Bouregy & Co., Inc.
160 Madison Avenue, New York, NY 10016

Library of Congress Cataloging-in-Publication Data

Cox, Connie, 1944–
    Taking flight / Connie Cox.
        p.   cm.
    ISBN 978-0-8034-9873-0 (acid-free paper)
    1. Air pilots--Fiction.   2. Louisiana--Fiction.   I. Title.

    PS3553.O916T35   2008
    813'.54—dc22
                                                    2007024972

PRINTED IN THE UNITED STATES OF AMERICA
ON ACID-FREE PAPER
BY HADDON CRAFTSMEN, BLOOMSBURG, PENNSYLVANIA

To Sissy: Home is where the bark is

Chapter One

The ground rushed up too fast toward the J3 Cub. Landing gear flexed and wheels gouged into the fresh-graded earth as the small plane slammed onto the iron-ore road. For a thousand feet the vintage plane skidded, kicking up a rooster tail of gravel and red dust.

Hank Chandler fought the controls, muscling the plane away from the irrigation ditches flanking him.

The Cub slowed to a stop with her nose just out of reach of the sawhorse blocking the road. The wind from her propeller ripped the hand-lettered sign from its staples. Road Closed For Cropduster floated into the newly fertilized field.

Blood charged with adrenaline finally reached his brain. He took a deep breath to slow the racing of his heart and the rushing of his mind. It was just chance that he'd touched down before his hands started to shake. He

1

hadn't had a hard landing like this one since he first started flying, over a decade ago.

He had been lucky, and he was grateful. Good luck, for him, didn't happen very often. He usually did things the hard way.

As his prop stopped its spin, he looked around to see who might have witnessed his embarrassment. The fields were just as deserted this afternoon as when he'd started spraying this morning.

Ignoring the tremor in his legs, he climbed from the cockpit and swiped off his ball cap. The purple-and-gold relic from his LSU days dripped from sweat. The machismo part of him blamed heat and humidity but the honest part held raw nerves responsible for the dampness of his T-shirt.

How could I have been so stupid? I'd been thinking about Lacey, worrying about seeing her after all these years, when I should have been worrying about getting this job done.

It was a stupid mistake, and he knew better. Mistakes and cropdusters don't mix.

A cool blast of May air raced over his skin, drying the sweat and raising goosebumps on his forearms. The wind blew from the north, creating thermals and an occasional downdraft. That's what had caught him. Not that the weather was uncommon. In fact, this time of year it was the norm.

What wasn't normal was Lacey coming home and Hank being here to see her again.

He walked around the plane and inspected for damage.

This plane was tough, like him, but he'd flown her down hot and hard. Squatting down, he ran his hand down the wheel strut. On the surface, she looked fine. If only people were as simple as airplanes.

His knees creaked as he stood, making him feel much older than his twenty-eight years. He kicked at a clump of red mud in the road and watched it roll, then bust into chunks. The knot in his stomach did the same.

How could he face her after all these years? For heaven's sake, she was the only woman who'd ever heard him cry.

The runway markers grew as the little turbo-prop plane approached Monroe Municipal Airport. With barely a screech of tires, the ATR touched down on the concrete runway.

As Lacey Seivers dug her fold-over garment bag from under the tiny seat, the pilot's voice scratched over the plane's intercom. "Welcome to Monroe, Louisiana, and thank you for flying our airline. The weather is a balmy eighty-five degrees with seventy-nine percent humidity, just right for steaming vegetables on the sidewalk."

Trying to ignore her claustrophobia, she waited her turn in the narrow aisle as the flight attendant opened the door and let down the stairs. Immediately, the air inside the plane became heavy.

After ten years of only Christmastime visits, she had lost her acclimation for north Louisiana in the spring.

Finally, she wobbled down the steep metal stairway, purse and carry-on garment bag precariously balanced over her left shoulder, jacket and computer satchel across her right arm. *Please don't let this grand homecoming start with a fall flat on my face.*

She'd sprung for a sophisticated French twist along with fresh blond highlights, a pair of sky-high wedges, and even a new SuperBra, all to make an impression and take the attention from the ten pounds she'd meant to loose. But slapstick comedienne wasn't exactly the impression she wanted to make.

Although she was a lot slimmer than she used to be in high school, she wasn't thin. Spending major dollars and hours at the gym, she'd attempted to work her butt off, literally, but somehow it never happened.

Although the air-conditioned terminal sat only three yards away, Lacey thought she might melt on the walk across the black asphalt tarmac. Perspiration tickled her temples and ran down her cheeks, tracing a trail in her carefully applied makeup.

The line in the women's restroom showed her that she might get a stall sometime next week.

Instead she found an open seat in the lobby and pulled her phone from her purse. The house phone rang to no avail. With any luck, Mom had picked up her voice message that she would be arriving a day early and would send someone to meet her. Lacey didn't need the lack of a taxi row to remind her that she wasn't in Chicago anymore.

Out of habit, she took a glance at her calendar, then grimaced at the week of vacation she had penciled in. She had been putting in fifteen hour days to clear her work calendar for this week, but she would still be behind when she returned.

Nevertheless, the trip would be worth the heat and the change in her schedule. Swapping her traditional Christmas vacation for one week in the middle of May would leave her alone in the cold Windy City over the holidays, but it wasn't every day that her twin brothers graduated from college. The family had known Zeb would sail through if he would only bother to show up for class, but Josh had surprised them all. Dismal freshman grades had evolved into cum laude status.

Compared to her parents' sacrifice to give them all the privilege to walk across the stage, diploma in hand, her sacrifice of switching vacations was nothing at all.

If she just didn't have to attend her darned ten-year high school reunion too.

When she had received the invitation and noted that it coincided with the twin's graduation, she knew she could never find an excuse that would satisfy her mother or her former classmates. So she started practicing yoga, mentally preparing herself for the jokes and giggles about fainting when she gave the valedictorian speech. And she kept reminding herself that she would be strutting into that reunion ball as a former nerd-girl turned big city success story. She had every reason to enjoy herself.

Then there was Hank.

The loud speaker blared that her flight's luggage would be delivered to the baggage carousel.

The single baggage carousel began its whirl, shooting out Lacey's suitcase first. She sprinted past a cluster of people and reached for the handle before the case could disappear through the return chute. As she bent over to snatch it, she felt the seams on her new jean skirt stretch and pull. It had looked trendy in the dressing room mirror but it was turning out to be a major lapse in judgment.

"Lacey Seivers? Is that you?" The woman's effervescent voice sounded familiar, but Lacey couldn't come up with a name. "Wow! I barely recognized you. What a change! You look great!"

Lacey dragged the overstuffed bag off the conveyor and let it fall to the floor. The handle took off the tip of a freshly sculpted and painted thumbnail.

Resisting the urge to suck her thumb, Lacey turned to see Heather Dixon, looking as beautiful as she had a decade ago. The only difference between now and then was the slight ball of a stomach under her maternity top.

Heather laid her perfectly manicured hand on Lacey's elbow. "I'm here to pick up Mitch for the reunion. Mitch has done very well for himself. Who would have ever thought . . . ? You know I'm on the invitation committee, don't you? Anyway, I was just thrilled when I saw your name on the RSVP list. We've got several out-of-towners coming. Won't it be fun to see everyone again?"

Still as bubbly as ever, the former high school cheerleader barely gave Lacey a chance to nod yes. Heather lowered her voice and leaned close, her light fragrance smelling clean and fresh compared to Lacey's airplane-stale sweat. "I noticed you only requested one ticket for the banquet. If you want, I can fix you up with a date. My cousin can always be pried away from the house, as long as wrestling's not on TV."

As the heat rose in Lacey's face, she searched frantically for a reply but words failed her, just like they used to in high school. Darn! All those years of training and she couldn't squeeze out a single sentence. Could she ever shed the geeky image everyone here had of her?

"Honey, I didn't mean to embarrass you." Heather looked puzzled but remorseful that she'd upset Lacey. Heather had used that same slightly bewildered but completely innocent expression to get out of trouble back in her high school years. She shrugged and patted her stomach. "I've got to run to the little girls' room. You know how it is—oops—I guess you don't. Sorry, again. Gotta go."

She probably wouldn't even have to wait her turn in line.

With a backward wave of her hand, she glided toward the restrooms, leaving Lacey alone amidst the jostling crowd.

Up ahead, a tall dark-haired man stepped from the coffee shop and joined the flow of traffic. Lacey's heart skipped a beat before she realized the man wasn't tall enough to be Hank. Hank had already topped six foot and his shoulders had filled a doorway by their senior year in high school.

She lugged her baggage to the airport pickup lane and waited at the curb for whomever Mom had talked into giving her a ride. As she dabbed at sweat with a soggy crumpled wad of napkin, she couldn't help but turn an envious eye on the graceful modern belles who glided past her into welcoming arms. Their rollerbags never twisted over in mid-pull and their clothes never wrinkled under the weight of their chic oversized, understuffed shoulderbags.

A screech of tires and a quick horn blast demanded her attention. Zeb hopped out of his truck and rushed to her, picking her up and twirling her around in as jubilant a hug as she could wish for.

"It's great to see you, sis."

"You too, Zeb. Graduating must agree with you. You definitely look smarter since I last saw you."

"I'll never be as smart as my big sister, will I, Ms. Big City Lawyer?" He wedged Lacey's bags between wooden crates and cardboard boxes in the bed of his truck.

"I don't know about that, Mr. Shrink. You might need to psychoanalyze me and find out."

"I'd need more than a psych degree to figure you out, Lace. That step's pretty high for you. Let me help you in." Without warning, Zeb swooped her up and lifted her over the muddy running boards of his jacked-up truck. "Hmmm. This is an excellent time to ask you something I've been wanting to know for a while now. Who's your favorite brother?"

Zeb held her securely around her waist, with her toes just out of reach of the ground.

Laughing, she said, "You are! You are! Now let me down." She settled onto the truck seat, grinning and giggling and lighter of heart than she had felt since the last time she was home.

"I've got to make one more stop at the FedEx dock, then we're homeward bound, okay?"

"Sure. I'm just along for the ride."

Zeb zoomed down the short block past the commercial hangars and pulled up outside a shipping dock. As soon as he slid from his seat and slammed shut his door, Lacey unbuckled and squirmed to pull down her creeping skirt. The truck's seatbelt gouged into her hip. She twisted to avoid the hunk of metal and ended up kicking her shoe under the bench seat.

But then, undressing in a truck wasn't something she'd had much practice with, unlike the girls who had hung on Hank's arm way back in high school. Reminding herself that her high school days were over and she was better for them kept her from feeling like that geeky misfit she had been as she wrenched at her hem.

Yes, this town had always made her feel fat, shy, and insecure, but she would let those anxieties flow through and past her. She took one deep, calming breath after another, willing her frustration to leave with each ohm.

Instead of inner calm, she ended up with a spinning head. Obviously watching yoga on TV wasn't enough to get her through moments like these.

But where TV yoga failed, bullheadedness would prevail. She had worked too hard to overcome her awkward shyness and insecurity to lose it all on her first day home. And she would not loose sight of her main goal.

Hank.

This week while she was home, she was determined to search for some flaw, some imperfection she could pin on him, just so the other guys didn't look so paltry in comparison.

She had to convince herself that the bigger-than-life image she'd built in her head didn't match the real thing. If nothing else, she was practical. Nobody could fulfill her idyllic fantasies of Hank. Not even the man himself.

Lacey licked her lips, then realized what she'd done. She dug into her purse until she found her new lipstick, a rich shade of red called Hearts on Fire. Squinting into her tiny compact mirror, she reapplied the color across her lips. She would have never worn such a bold shade in high school.

She'd have to keep reminding herself that she'd changed in more than looks.

What would Hank think of her now?

The driver's door opened and Zeb slid behind the wheel, interrupting the spiral her thoughts had slid down too many times.

He grimaced at her makeup collection laid across his dashboard. "Did I remember to say welcome home, sis? I guess you'll start hanging your underwear over the shower curtain bar again, huh?"

"Yeah and I plan to use up all the hot water and towels when I wash my hair, too. Just like old times."

Tonight, after supper, she would run across the field and throw rocks at Hank's bedroom window to get him to come out and look at the stars with her, just like old times. Then she'd let the old times go.

As Zeb took a corner too fast, she grabbed for the dashboard. She had dwelled on Hank long enough. Now she would just worry about getting home in one piece.

What would Lacey think of him now?

Hank brushed red dust from the knees of his jeans, then resettled his ballcap.

Over the phone, Lacey sounded the same as the day she'd left for Notre Dame, full academic scholarship in hand. No big time lawyer talk, just conversation between friends. What did she look like now? Of course, they'd all gotten a bit older, but had she changed where it counted?

Naw, Lacey would never change. She would be as sweet as ever.

Hank rubbed his hand across his late afternoon stubble. *He* certainly wasn't the same. He had Cody to thank for that.

The sound of Old Man Dalton's truck bouncing down the road toward him pulled him from his brooding. As the rusted green Ford slowed to a stop, Hank finished jotting down the amount of fertilizer he'd sprayed and put his logbook back into the cockpit. Dalton slid from the seat and trotted past the still prop. He stuck one hand out to Hank and patted the plane with the other.

"Got her done?" Dalton looked out at his fields, clearly pleased with the newly turned mounds of rich brown soil.

"Yup. All finished. Let me know how the new mix does."

"I will." Dalton leaned over and spat a wad of chewing tobacco into the ditch. "The thing is, Hank, I'm a little short on cash right now. Can you let me slide a month or so?"

"You'll have to talk to Glenna Seivers about money. All I do is fly the plane." Not for the first time, Hank gave thanks that Glenna took care of the billing. Lacey's mother could squeeze blood out of a turnip, and do it with such grace the turnip was grateful to give.

"I'll call her first thing when I get back to the house." Dalton stuck another wad of Copenhagen in his jaw.

"I'd better be getting back myself. Good luck with the crop this year."

The truck puttered back the way it had come and Hank watched it go, remembering when Dalton wouldn't give him the time of day. Yup, he'd changed. Mostly for the better, he hoped.

With the roadway clear, Hank grabbed a blade of the prop and spun it. The engine caught and roared to life.

The powerful sound put a smile on his face. How many men got to live their dream? He wasn't much for poetry but the guy who wrote the bit about "slipped the surly bonds of earth" knew what he was talking about.

Hank punched in Billy Seivers' number on his cell phone. After three rings, Billy answered.

"Hello, Billy? I had a hard landing, and I need to check her out. Can you bring the tractor?"

Hoping the static was an affirmative, Hank signed off and headed for home, determined not to think about Lacey.

That good intention lasted half a second.

A decade was a long time to go without seeing your best friend. Of course, there was the phone. That safe, insulating phone cord that had stretched between them for so many years had kept them apart as much as it tied them together.

Hank mentally squirmed when he thought about all the confidences he'd shared. Lacey alone knew his doubts, his frustrations, his fear of raising his son alone, all the things he kept hidden from a town that insisted he'd made the wrong decisions ten years ago.

Those had been dark days. He'd dumped all his worries on Lacey and she'd been his anchor, his security blanket, and his sanity. The worst had been the night of his nineteenth birthday. Cody had been home from the hospital for less than a week. Hank had walked the floor, phone cradled on one shoulder, colicky baby on the other, both father and son in tears.

Lacey had talked to him for hours, leading him through his desperation and panic, until they'd all slept from exhaustion.

Even after all these years, Hank still squirmed when he thought back on that night and how pathetic he'd been over the phone.

After the colic fiasco, he had planned a December visit to his mother and brother in Gulf Shores for the Christmas holidays so he could avoid an awkward encounter with Lacey during her semester break. One year had stretched into another, and he'd made a tradition of visiting his family during Christmas vacation while Lacey visited her own family. The phone calls had come fewer and farther between as she got on with her life and he got on with his and Cody's.

Looking back, she'd been his sounding board, his vote of confidence during those early years of fatherhood. As he matured, he'd worked hard to learn a few things and he'd needed her reassurance to talk him through his panic attacks less and less.

When was the last time he'd called? Early spring? They'd left a few messages back and forth since then but they both seemed to stay too busy. Besides, they had started running out of things to talk about. They had so little in common anymore, not like when they lived next door to each other.

Now that she was home again, what would he say to her? *I'm not the pathetic guy I sounded like way back then.* Not in this lifetime!

He'd have to come up with something. He owed it to their old friendship to put his shy, little, best buddy at ease.

Down below he saw Billy's old tractor sitting on the edge of their grass landing strip.

Ever so carefully, Hank executed a perfect landing.

Billy slid off the tractor seat, took his ever-present sucker from his mouth, and yelled over the roar of the motor. "Are you all right?"

Hank scrubbed his hand across the back of his neck, feeling like ten kinds of a fool. "I'm fine. I just set her down a little hard."

"That's not like you."

"I don't mean to make a habit of it."

Crawling back into the cockpit, Hank steered the plane across the field to Billy's shop. His Cub, so graceful in the air, bucked and hopped at the end of her tether as the tractor lurched along the path beaten into the tall grass.

Outside the shop, Cody and B.J. waited. Although B.J. was younger by three months, he topped Cody by several inches. He'd inherited his seriousness from Billy and his kindness from Glenna. The boys had more in common than being best friends. They'd both been surprise packages and both boys were the greatest gifts their fathers could ever imagine.

"What happened, Dad?" Cody hopped from one foot to the other, his thick glasses sliding further down his nose with each bounce.

The concern in Cody's eyes hit Hank in the gut. "Just a hard landing, son. Nothing to worry about."

"Oh. Okay." Cody pushed his fly-away blond hair from his sky-blue eyes, both legacies from his mother. Plenty of folks had made guesses, but her identity was a secret Hank had sworn to uphold. He would have promised anything to keep his son.

And Lacey had sworn that she'd go to the grave before telling anyone.

With Hank positioned behind one fabric-covered wing and the boys behind the other, they pushed the plane into the shop next to a two-seater RV-8 under construction. The shop, larger than three airplane hangers, held all the tools Billy needed to work on Hank's cropduster and the trainers from Louisiana Tech's flight school, with room left over for building an experimental airplane or two. While full with shelves and machinery from concrete floor to open-railed rafters, the shop was organized and freshly swept. Billy's only nod to aesthetics was his acrylic-on-velvet portrait of John Wayne over his main workbench. Box fans in the rafters circulated the air but drove the noise level inside the cavernous building to a dull roar.

Hank grabbed his flashlight and slid underneath the belly of his plane, praying she wasn't damaged. A full schedule of fourteen-hour days stretched before him and he didn't have room on the calendar for downtime.

As he settled in, the phone rang. Above the noise, Billy hollered, "One of you boys get that. I'm elbow deep in oil."

A few seconds later, B.J. called back, "Pop? Mom said to tell you that Zeb went to the airport to pick up Lacey. She took an earlier flight. He'll check on your parts while he's there."

Lacey was on her way? Hank focused all his concentration on the struts. Methodically, he trained the flashlight beam down the metal tubing and craned his neck to get a better look at the landing gear. Everything looked fine. Not even a bungee cord popped.

"Dad? Dad! Ms. Glenna says we can ride the tractor if you or Mr. Billy will crank it."

Out of the corner of his eye, Hank saw Cody's tennis shoes bouncing near his own outstretched feet. With every jump, the rubber sole of his tennis shoes pulled away from the dirt-stained nylon. Those shoes were less than two months old and they looked like they were ready for the trash can. Grease stained his jeans and a quarter-sized hole showed a scraped knee.

Hank inspected his son as an outsider might. Hair too long, clothes dirty and ragged. *What would Lacey think?* After all these years of encouragement, would she decide that all the busybodies were right and he was a bad parent?

"Hey, Billy, she looks okay to me, but I'd like your opinion when you get a chance."

"Sure, Hank. I'll look her over when I'm done breaking loose these bolts."

"Da-ad. Can we ride the tractor *now*?" Cody's voice hit that strident frequency that only a nine-year-old can reach. He karate-chopped an invisible foe. "I wanna ride first since it was my idea. Can we, Dad?"

B.J. faked a roundhouse kick that sent his untied tennis shoe flying. "I wonder what Lacey's gonna bring me this time? I've already gotten to level twelve on the UltraRat game she gave me at Christmas."

"How come I've never gotten to meet Lacey?" Cody challenged Hank with a glare, as if his dad had kept this magnanimous gift bearer from him on purpose.

"Because we're always at Gramma's during Christmas and that's when Lacey comes home." *Should I try to trim his hair myself, or would that only make it worse?* "Now, come on. I've got to get you into the tub." Hank's guilty conscience made his voice sharper than he had intended.

"But, Dad, the tractor . . ."

"I don't have to take a bath, do I, Pop?" B.J. sidled up to Billy. "It's just Lacey. And I'm not as dirty as you are, huh?"

Billy looked down at his oily T-shirt and jeans and sent Hank an apologetic look. "I don't really have time to stop work and clean up just because Lacey's getting here early. I've got to get these mags calibrated before the game tonight."

"Dad? Please?" Cody pushed his glasses up and peered at Hank through his too-long bangs.

I'm twenty-eight years old, for goodness' sake. I don't need to prove myself to anyone anymore. Especially not to Lacey, the only person in the world who never judged me. "All right, Cody. I'll get the tractor going for you."

In a stare as serious as The Duke's, Billy narrowed his eyes through his safety glasses. "B.J., I better not catch you putting that blade down again to write your name in the grass. It took me three cuttings to get your mother's lawn back to normal."

"Okay, Pop. C'mon, Cody." B.J. ran for the shop door, paying as little attention to Billy's bluster as Lacey had at that age.

Routinely, Hank checked the oil and fuel mixture and began to wipe down the windshield. In the distance, he halfway listened to Cody and B.J. arguing about who got to drive first. How many years had it been since he and Lacey fought that same fight? They'd spent hours together driving the tractor, fishing in the creek, or just lying in the grass, listening to it grow. He'd watched the shifting clouds and fantasized about baseball and fame. Lacey had dreamed of big cities and business suits. They'd spat in each other's palms and promised to be best buddies forever. But forever was a long time and nothing had turned out the way he'd planned.

Instead of leaving LSU as a pro ballplayer, he'd left as a flunked out freshman. His truck had been packed to overflowing with all the stuff he'd dragged to his frat house two semesters earlier, his preemie newborn's car seat strapped front and center. Within seven months, the dreams of an eighteen-year-old college student had changed into the nightmares of a single father and provider.

His dreams might not have come true like Lacey's did, but he hadn't done too badly. He owned his own plane, free and clear, except for the motor. The bank still had a larger stake in his new Continental 90 horse-power bundle of joy than he did, but if this season was a good one he might burn the note by year's end.

The high-pitched whine of mud grips on pavement caught his attention. He wiped off his hands and stood in the shade of the deep sheet metal overhang fronting the shop.

Billy, elbow-deep in oil, called from his workbench, "Is that Zeb with the parts?"

"Looks like it."

The truck turned off the road and bounced down the drive, spewing gravel and asphalt shingle tabs in its wake.

Hank squinted to see past the tinted windows into the cab. "That isn't Lacey with him, is it?"

As if in response, the passenger door opened and a pair of bare legs a mile long slithered from the tall truck.

Chapter Two

Lacey slid from the truck seat and scrunched her bare toes against the hot, scratchy shingle tab driveway.

From her father's shop, the clinks and clunks of metal against metal punctuated the country music that always played from Pop's tinny AM radio. The rhythmic twang from the cheap portable radio moved her like no symphonic movement ever could. She tugged at her skirt, bunched high on her thighs from the slide off the seat, and bent to retrieve her shoes from the truck's floorboard.

One shoe lay in easy reach and she grabbed it and forced it over her sweaty foot. But the other shoe peeped from deep under the seat, next to an old candy bar wrapper. Stretching from tiptoes to fingertips, she reached—just a half-inch more—and snagged her other shoe.

Her new bra's underwire rode up, pinching tender

skin. A breeze cooled the back of her thighs, making her grateful she was among family.

"How you doing, Lacey?" Hank's rich voice throbbed through her like a bass guitar cranked up too loud.

She felt, rather than heard, his words as they dropped into the pit of her stomach.

"I'm fine, Hank. Just fine." She grabbed her skirt hem, yanking it down as she backed out of the truck. *So much for making a graceful entry.*

Still, here was the moment she'd been looking forward to and dreading ever since she'd bought her plane tickets.

With resolve in place, she turned to face him, ready and willing to deflate her overblown memories.

Her shoe fell from limp fingers to bounce on the shingle tabs.

Her imagination had failed her. This grown-up version of Hank was so much more than the teenager she'd last seen.

The world stopped turning as she watched him bend down to fish for her shoe under the truck.

While he knelt at her feet, she took advantage of the view.

Dark-brown hair the color of a Nestle's chocolate bar curled down his neck, just touching the neckband of his faded black T-shirt. Corded muscles stood in bas-relief on his thick forearms as he reached for the shoe. Soft, faded jeans hugged his strong, athletic thighs.

Then he looked up to catch her staring at him and grinned, just a slight upward quirk of those sensuous lips, just enough to show his dimple, just enough to steal away her last breath.

She dropped her gaze to his feet, only to be reminded of her toes, bare except for the red nail polish and silver toe ring. She covered one foot with the other. Even as she felt her cheeks flush, she berated herself. Being embarrassed about bare feet was just plain silly. Hank had seen her more often without shoes than with them.

With eyes still downcast on her scrunched toes, Lacey peeked at Hank through her eyelashes.

He caught her bare foot in his hand. His callused thumb brushed across her arch while his long, strong fingers encircled her ankle.

Shivers ran from her toes, straight to her heart, making all her nerve endings tingle on the way up.

"You okay?" His voice hadn't made her spine vibrate like this over the phone.

Blurting out "no" wouldn't do at all.

She'd been trained to think fast on her feet, but not standing storklike on one foot. "Your hand tickles."

Hopefully, her choked answer sounded more like she fought back a giggle fit instead of a panic attack.

He cradled her shoe onto her foot, then stood, trapping her between the truck and himself.

She forgot to breathe. Her gasp for air drew searing heat into her lungs. This heat wasn't caused by the weather.

"Hey, Pop! I could use some help out here," Zeb hollered toward the shop, shaking Lacey out of the spell Hank had woven around her.

Hank blinked as if he, too, had been caught up in the trance.

What had she been thinking? She reached to pat him on the arm as he attempted to give her a one-armed hug and she ended up with her fist crammed into his armpit. She halfway buried her face in his shirt, until he awkwardly unwrapped from her. With a wink a shade more embarrassed than cocky, he swung himself into the back of Zeb's truck and went to work unknotting one of the ropes that held the crates and boxes.

She breathed in the all-male scent of him and slowly released it.

For heaven's sake, this was Hank, her childhood friend. This awareness—this attraction—was a silly crush, one she should have outgrown back in high school. This was not going at all as planned.

Billy stepped out from underneath the shop's deep overhang. "Well, don't you look beautiful, baby girl."

Refuge—finally! "'Lo, Pop! I'm home!" Lacey grinned at her father as he hustled toward her. "Where's my hug?"

"I'll get you dirty." He held up his hands to show the grease staining his shirt.

"I'm not made of sugar. I'll wash." She melted into his strong bear hug, burying her face in his chest. Even safe in her father's arms, she felt the hairs on her neck crawl, knowing Hank stood only three feet away.

She *had* to find that comfortable friendship with him before she broke out in hives.

"Welcome home, sweetie." Billy lifted her up and

twirled her around before setting her on her feet. "You're a day early. I'd have picked you up in your mother's car if I'd known you were coming in today."

"That's all right. I'm glad to be home any way I could get here." The deep truth of those words brought tears to Lacey's eyes. She hadn't realized how much she'd missed home. But she wouldn't cry. Her mascara would run down to her chin. "I worked late last night and got caught up, so I decided to take a chance on standby and was able to catch an earlier flight this morning. I'm just lucky to get here in one piece with Zeb's kamikaze driving skills."

From behind a big box, Zeb called, "You're welcome."

Billy gave his daughter another twirl, then set her on her feet. "Let me help Zeb get these boxes unloaded, then I'll carry your things to the house."

"I only brought necessities, Pop, one suitcase and a couple of dresses in the carry-on." She pointed to the wheeled suitcase and the fold-over garment bag draped across a cardboard box in the truck bed.

"Necessities, huh?" Billy eyed the bulging suitcase and carry-on. "I thought your mother was making your outfit for the dance?"

"That's my dress for the graduation and another one, just in case. Plus, I need the garment bag to carry the evening gown that Momma's made for me back to Chicago."

He chomped his sucker and shook his head. "From what I've seen of that reunion dress, it won't take up too much room in your luggage."

"If you had your way, Pop, I'd wear mechanic's overalls zipped all the way to my throat."

"It would certainly get you an extra look or two at the dance, wouldn't it, baby girl?" He shielded his eyes against the sun as he looked toward the truck. "What do you think, Hank?"

Hank didn't even look their way as he untangled another knot. "I'm not paid to think, just to unload boxes."

"That's what I like about you. You know when to be a silent partner." Billy took the crate from Hank and headed toward the shop, but called over his shoulder, "But then, you're not too overworked to appreciate a pretty girl, are you?"

Hank's answer was a noncommittal grunt.

Lacey couldn't help but wonder who Hank had asked to the reunion dance. No doubt, he had his pick of dozens of willing women. To get a grip, Lacey took a deep breath. The air smelled like no other. West Monroe and insecurity burned her lungs.

Funny how the more things changed, the more they stayed the same.

The smell of diesel exhaust and the sputter-chug of the old Massey-Ferguson motor alerted Lacey to the ancient tractor barreling down on her. Running a hundred yards behind the old tractor, a boy yelled, "Slow down, B.J., wait for me."

Gears screamed in protest as her youngest brother downshifted to a stop. Beaming with success, B.J. jumped from the tractor seat and ran to his sister. "Hey, Lacey. You're home!"

"How you been, Beej? Looks like you've grown another foot."

B.J. stared down at his tennis shoes before giving his sister a cheeky grin. "Nope, still got just two of them. But look at this." B.J. held up his arm, Popeye style, to show his growing strength.

Even as she squeezed his flexed muscle and murmured praise, she watched Hank, unable to stop herself. From the corner of her eye, she saw him stand and stretch, flexing his arms high over his head.

B.J. swaggered toward the truck, intercepting her line of sight. "Want me to get your stuff? I can carry it."

Hank reached out a hand to B.J. "Grab hold." With a one-handed tug, he pulled B.J. into the truck.

Lacey's mouth went dry. It was just as well. If she could have swallowed right then, she would have swallowed her tongue.

Zeb called over the top of a box, "Did you hear her, Pop? Just half an hour ago, she claimed I was the best brother in the world."

"*He's* the best brother in the world? What about me?" From his perch on the tailgate, B.J. dropped her garment bag, not noticing that it crumpled to the ground. As B.J. jumped from the truck bed, Hank leaned over the tailgate and picked up the mistreated bag.

B.J. watched Lacey with an expectant look. What had her littlest brother asked her? Oh, yeah. The best brother thing.

"Zeb made me say it, B.J. He held me in the air so my feet wouldn't touch until I told him he was the best.

Don't worry, though. I said it under coercion so it doesn't count."

She almost fell on her face as B.J. hurtled into her. He wrapped his arms around her and squeezed her in the tightest hold he could manage.

"B.J., you're squashing me. What are you doing?"

"I'm gonna pick you up like Zeb and Pop do." B.J. tugged and heaved until Lacey relented and stood on her tiptoes for him.

Grinning from ear to ear, he thrust out his chest. "See, Zeb. I'm almost as strong as you are."

"Yup, you're really strong to be able to lift Lacey under the weight of all that hairspray she's wearing." Zeb crossed his eyes at Lacey, and she stuck her tongue out at him.

B.J. jumped in front of her, intercepting her line of vision. "I want you to meet my best friend." B.J. pointed toward the shop overhang to the boy who had chased the tractor and now stood in the shade. "C'mon out and meet my sister!" B.J. yelled to the boy standing in the shadows of the awning catching his breath.

B.J. dragged Cody from under the awning, pulling on his arm like he would pull it from the socket. "Come on, Cody. You want to try? She's not that heavy."

Lacey looked into her brother's earnest eyes and tried to hold back her laugh. "Thanks, B.J. I try not to be."

Obviously inspired by B.J.'s encouragement, Cody rushed toward the truck, stopping short inches from Lacey's toes. Without saying a word, he examined her from her upswept hairdo to her designer shoes. Then he pushed his glasses up with one finger and took a deep breath, obviously readying himself for the lift.

Quickly, Lacey thrust out her hand. "I'm Lacey, B.J.'s sister. Would a handshake do instead?"

By the sudden droop of his chin, the boy showed his disappointment that his weightlifting attempt had been thwarted. Shrugging his bony shoulders, he took Lacey's proffered hand. "I'm Cody."

"Nice to meet you, Cody." He shared Hank's dimple. The slight indention looked so innocent on Hank's son. Nothing about Hank had looked innocent since he had turned fourteen.

Cody nodded yes. Then his eyes lit up. "Dad's very strong. I'll bet he could do it!"

Cody yelled at his father as Hank carried his load from the truck. "Dad! Lacey wants you to pick her up! I told her you would."

Lacey's face flamed worse than the first sunburn of summer. She heard a strangling noise, as if Hank had swallowed a bug.

Arms full of crate, Hank explored Lacey with his eyes. Lacey wanted to believe it was admiration she saw reflected in those deep brown irises.

Hank shifted the crate. "I've got my hands full now. Maybe another time."

That voice. Hank's voice. It flowed like warm ribbon cane syrup. What Lacey wouldn't give to be a tall stack of homemade pancakes!

Hank gawked as Lacey strolled across the yard on legs that would make a supermodel cry. That wasn't his best buddy. That was a . . . a woman! . . . and a full grown one, to boot. Who was this elegant, uptown lady who oozed grace and style? And what had she done with his best friend?

This was the stranger he'd poured out his soul to? His hands still trembled from touching her foot, for heaven's sake.

He must have seemed like an old blind coondog, sniffing around her like that.

And wouldn't it have been something if he'd dropped that three hundred dollar, custom-machined part he'd been carrying when his own son had suggested he carry Lacey instead?

With the old Lacey, the one he thought he'd been talking to all these years, he'd have thrown her over his shoulder, caveman style, until her distant reserve dissolved into giggles. But this Lacey, this woman who barely spoke to him, he didn't even dare touch again without her permission.

Hank watched her walk toward the house, picking her way through the grass on her high heels. Her hips swayed as she climbed the three short concrete steps to the screened-in porch.

Billy still watched Glenna the same way, even after thirty years of marriage. He'd say, "Wish I had that swing in my backyard." Then he'd chuckle and say, "Well, aren't I a lucky man. I guess I do." And every time, Hank wished he were lucky too.

But this was Lacey, a Lacey he didn't know, and he had no business thinking about her like that at all.

A nail shrieked in protest as Zeb pulled it from the wooden crate. Hank grimaced at the noise as it grated along his raw nerve endings.

He stooped to pick up the nail Zeb had sprung across the concrete floor and, against his better judgment, asked anyway, "Did Lacey seem a little distracted to you?"

Zeb shot him an assessing look that reminded Hank that Zeb's major was psychology. "A little. But then, so did you. You hardly said two words to her."

"I didn't want to get in the way of family." Hank closed his toolbox and set it on the workbench. "Speaking of family, it's about time Cody and I headed for the house. I need to feed him before the game tonight."

"You know you're family, you and Cody both."

"Thanks, Zeb," Hank said around the lump in his throat. He stuck his baseball cap on his head and looked out at his son bouncing on the tractor seat. "I better round up Cody. See you at the ballpark."

"You bet."

Scents of wood polish, pine cleaner, and hot biscuits wrapped around Lacey like a security blanket. Through the oven door, Lacey saw brownies beginning to set.

"Hey, Lacey, you're home." The deep voice of her brother Josh came from under the chrome-and-Formica dinette set.

"Josh? What are you doing under there?" Lacey bent down to stare at her brother, all six foot three inches of him contorted under the table. The opposite of his twin Zeb in every way, Josh was the classic super jock.

Although he was honey-blond and green-eyed like her, that's where the family resemblance ended. But then, none of her brothers had ever had a problem with being a geek like their big sister.

Josh grinned and unfolded himself from under the table. "The boys and I were making you a Welcome Home sign, but we spilt the glitter."

Lacey's mom walked into the kitchen, a stack of folded dishtowels in her hand. "They didn't spill the glitter. They blew it all over my kitchen. Josh convinced them that they could make swirls with the blow dryer."

"Did you miss me, Mom?"

"Of course I did, honey." Glenna enfolded Lacey in an embrace that smelled of baking and felt like home.

"I saw Pop and Hank at the shop before I walked up. They seemed to be busy."

"Hank had a problem with his plane. That's probably what they're working on." Glenna bent to pull the brownies from the oven, missing Lacey's worried frown. "You're in luck! The boys' baseball season kicks off tonight with the parents' game. Since you're here early, you can play for me."

Lacey scarcely heard her mother's second remark. The one about Hank's plane captured all her attention. "What kind of problem?"

Josh rubbed his sister's shoulder as he reached past her to grab a biscuit from the pan resting on the potholder on the counter. "Just a hard landing. It happens sometimes. No harm done, though."

Lacey smiled at her brother, hearing reassurance in his voice. She snagged her own biscuit and breathed deeply, savoring the smell of hot bread and butter. As she bit into the biscuit, she realized what else her mom had said and the biscuit became nothing more than a lump of hard dough. Baseball was the one thing in her life that made her feel like a total loser, the one thing that had kept her from her best buddy as they were growing up.

"You want me to play baseball? But I haven't played in years and I'm not a parent, Mom. I don't even know what a parents' game is."

Josh answered for his mother, talking around the hot biscuit he just plopped into his mouth. "The first game of the season, the parents have to play in their kids' places. It's supposed to keep the parents from jumping on their kids when they screw up."

Glenna put the biscuits into a bowl, swatting at her son's hand as he tried to grab another one. "Your pop is playing on my team, but I have to umpire so I need someone to take my place."

"But Momma, I haven't played baseball since eighth grade." Lacey's whine sounded pitiful to her own ears. "I don't even know where my glove is."

Josh sponged up the rest of the glitter, wiping a bit of sparkle on his sister's nose. "It's probably in that box of equipment in the storeroom. Remember when Momma loaded us into the car and took us all down to Wal-Mart to buy gloves? When I put that first glove on, I felt like such a big kid—just like you and Hank." He held up his massive palm and wiggled his fingers. "It's so small now, I can't get it on my hand."

Lacey well remembered buying those first gloves. She'd been determined to find out why Hank waxed so enthusiastic about the game. He had talked of nothing but line drives and stolen bases. Everyone who was anyone in West Monroe played baseball. And she really, really wanted to be someone, especially in Hank's eyes.

Shy and awkward at nine, she'd felt like an outsider trying to fit in, even among the kids she'd known since kindergarten.

Not only had she not made the team, she hadn't even made the draft picks. The league didn't have enough volunteer coaches for those at the bottom of the list.

One of the kids had laughed at her and convinced the rest of the kids to join in. Hank had punched him, then he'd gotten into big trouble for fighting and everyone found out about it.

She'd come home mortified.

Until the valedictorian incident, it had been the most embarrassing moment in her life.

Glenna had wiped away her daughter's tears of embarrassment and coerced Billy into mowing a portion of the back pasture so the family could all play catch together. Then her mom volunteered to coach so Lacey would have a team to play for.

How many hours had Glenna spent pouring over the rulebook? Her mother, who had thought diamonds were only for engagement rings, immersed herself in the science of baseball so she could teach it to a bunch of clumsy children. And she'd coached every year since then, to make sure that each of her children had a turn in the batter's box. Not that Zeb, Josh, or B.J. fell anywhere near the bottom of the list like Lacey had.

Lacey wouldn't let her mom down now. And she shouldn't let herself down either. What did it matter that she had neither grace nor aptitude on the diamond? She would show everyone that she was somebody, athlete or not, right?

"Sure, I'll play ball for you, Mom."

Glenna kissed her on the cheek. "Thanks, honey. I can always count on you."

"Great! With Hank and I on one team and you and Dad on the other, it will be a shut out." Josh stole another biscuit and chanted with his mouth full, "We're gonna beat you. We're gonna beat you."

"But if I'm playing on Mom's team, why aren't you?"

" 'Cause I get to play on the good team." Josh gave her a cheeky grin. "This year, Mom and Hank decided it would be better for the boys if they didn't coach their own kids. And Zeb is Hank's assistant coach. Since B.J. is on Hank's team, Zeb and I are playing for B.J. You and Pop will be playing for Cody."

Hank's team? Hank would be there? Her bravado drained away. *What if I embarrass myself in front of everyone I've ever tried to impress?*

All Lacey's hard-earned grace and poise melted away in memories of strikeouts and lonely hours in right field.

Now, her first day in town, her confidence would be shattered like a baseball through a plate-glass window. And Hank would have a box seat to watch the shards fall. Without a doubt, she'd get cut. She just hoped she wouldn't bleed too much in public.

Chapter Three

Hank nuked leftover spaghetti while Cody washed up then set the table. Cody hadn't said two words since they'd left the Seivers', a sure sign that he was thinking hard on something. He slurped up a noodle, letting it dangle a second or two, then got down to the business of interrogation.

"Dad, Lacey doesn't look like she does in those pictures on your dresser. In the one where you were hugging on her, she had a big smile that made her eyes squint. And in the other one, she was holding up a certificate."

"For straight A's all through grade school. Lacey's always been brilliant. Now drink your milk and finish up or we'll be late."

Cody stopped chewing and got real quiet.

"Did you make all A's, Dad?"

Hank gave his son a sympathetic look. "No, son. I didn't."

"Math is hard isn't it, Dad."

"You have to hang in there, Cody. You've got to get it figured out." Hank thought back to all the tutoring Lacey used to give him. His teachers, his parents, even his older brother couldn't make the numbers add up for him. When everyone else despaired, Lacey had always found the words to pull him through.

Hank smiled. Who would have thought that meek, quiet little Lacey would end up being an attorney. And a good one, too, according to the success stories Glenda passed on to him. She had almost refused to be valedictorian because she was afraid to speak in public. She must have changed as much on the inside as she did on the outside.

"What are you grinning about, Dad?"

"Just thinking about Lacey."

"Were you and Lacey ever girlfriend-and-boyfriend?"

"No, we were more. We were best friends."

"Oh." Cody considered the levels of friendship for a moment. "B.J. is my best friend."

"Best friends are important."

"Why aren't you and Lacey best friends anymore?"

Hank's last bite of spaghetti stuck in his throat. How could he explain to a child when he wasn't sure himself? "I let unimportant things get in the way."

"Like girlfriends? Because B.J. said he likes Winnie Griggs and he ate lunch with her every day last week and I had to eat by myself. I finally decided to sit with Mike because he was all by himself too."

Hank mentally apologized for underestimating his son. Cody did understand. "Yeah, like that."

Hank wished he had had Cody's wisdom back then. Had Lacey looked at him with big, sad eyes when he deserted her at lunch?

"You're not gonna get a girlfriend, are you, Dad?" Cody couldn't have made his worries more clear if he had out-and-out asked if his dad would abandom him should Hank start seriously dating. No wonder Cody resented everyone, especially women, that Hank spent time with. Thankfully, the Seivers were exempt. Hank just wished he'd had a clue a few years ago. But then, the older Cody got, the smarter Hank had to get to keep up with all his questions and he might not have had the answer then.

"No matter how many friends I get, Cody, I'll always be your dad. You are the most important person in my life and I will never, ever let anyone get in the way of us."

Cody's eyes bored into Hank's as if Cody was trying to look into Hank's soul. "I love you, Dad."

"I love you, too, son."

The screen door slammed open, startling Lacey from her gloomy ponderings about revisiting the baseball diamond. B.J. huffed and puffed as he dragged her suitcase behind him across the kitchen floor.

Rescuing the bag from her littlest brother, she made her way down the hall to her room—her sanctuary.

She pushed open her bedroom door and walked back in time. Inhaling peace, Lacey exhaled all her worries.

She was home. Not a couple of rooms she paid rent for, but real, true home. The cramped room, dominated by shades of pink and turquoise, fit her better than her spacious navy and burgundy apartment ever would. No one and nothing could take away the sense of belonging she felt when she entered her room.

She slung her coat over the three-foot-tall stuffed chartreuse poodle Hank had won for her at the fair when they had been twelve. That was the summer before junior high; the summer before Hank noticed other girls noticing him.

After that, she became plain ole Lacey. She couldn't begin to compete with beautiful, teeth-straightened, junior high cheerleader, Gina Mae Davis. When Hank gave Gina Mae the gold fish he won at the First Baptist Church's Fall Festival, Lacey locked herself in the bathroom and cried.

A box of tissues later, Lacey realized that she could still be Hank's friend, even if she would never be his girlfriend. And she considered each whispered confidence a gem. The ones about other girls were a little harder to treasure, but she took the dross with the gold. At least it glittered.

But Hank would never know.

She wanted to see *passion*, not *compassion* in those dark chocolate eyes. She'd rather bear her unrequited love the rest of her lonely life than see pity in Hank's eyes.

Lacey laughed at herself for her melodrama.

Now she was home and being lonely was out of the question. Her biggest problem this week would be getting enough time in the bathroom to shave her legs.

Hank checked the fit of his baseball pants in his bedroom mirror. Ten years old and faded, they were a bit more snug than they had been the last time Lacey had seen him wear them. What would she think—if she thought anything at all?

As if it mattered. To her, he was Hank, the boy who still lived next door in the same house he'd grown up in. She probably went for the polished, sophisticated types who never had grease under their fingernails and who knew which wine to order with their dinner entrées.

"C'mon, Dad. We're gonna be late." The front door slammed on Cody's words as his son ran outside.

Hank glanced at the clock, grabbed his ball cap and headed for the door. Two steps back, he checked the angle of the cap in the mirror frowning at the creases bracketing his eyes. He was too old for vanity and way too old to worry about what Lacey, or any other woman, thought about his looks. Besides, he had enough to do in his life without adding the complications of courting a woman.

Why, when he thought about courting, had Lacey come to mind? She was his business partner's daughter and his best friend, for heaven's sake. That was more than enough of a relationship for a man with a nine-year-old to raise.

On a whim, he squirted himself with cologne then rushed out to join Cody in his truck.

Lacey unpacked her single suitcase and hung up her royal blue silk dress. She had searched for days for a dress that clung in the right places and flowed over others. Just maybe she would run into someone who remembered when she would have looked like a stuffed sausage in a dress. Just maybe that someone would be Hank.

No, Hank wouldn't notice if she wore a Hefty garbage sack. Just like in the good ole days.

She reached for the jeans hanging in her closet, then drew her hand back. She'd been hitting the Chicago pizza hard the last month or so. Would it show? Leaving the top button undone felt so tacky. It was a sure bet that none of Hank's women had ever had to resort to such measures.

A knock on the door broke into her musings. "Lacey, I brought you a pair of Zeb's old baseball pants. If they won't do, I've got some gym shorts that might work." Glenna opened the door a crack and held out the clothes, complete with long white socks. "Game time's in an hour."

Lacey eyed the polyester knit baseball pants, then the onionskin running shorts. And she had been worried about denim?

After trying on both choices, she opted for the pants. They hugged her legs like a second skin but at least she didn't feel exposed. She looked for her longest T-shirt, settling on a freebie that advertised airplane parts.

Remembering how sweat could make mascara burn like the fires of hell, she headed to the bathroom to scrub her face clean.

A jiggle of the knob proved the door was locked. "Hey, who's in there? Are you drowning or what?" Lacey banged on the bathroom door, realizing how easily old phrases skipped off her tongue.

She never had to share her bathroom in Chicago. She had never found anyone worth sharing with.

Who had time to date, anyway? She was busy building her career. If she stayed late at the office on Friday nights, it wasn't that she didn't have anything better to do. She just had to tie up loose ends before the weekend.

All her hard work was only a few weeks away from paying off.

Josh, enveloped in steam, emerged from the bathroom. "All yours, sis." Then he gave her a big hug. "I'm glad you're home."

How could she gripe at him after that?

She turned on the spigot and waited for the hot water until she realized there wasn't any. Grimacing as she splashed icy water on her face, she rinsed away her makeup. Then she combed out her French twist and pulled her hair into a ponytail.

Lacey looked in the mirror with dismay. Ten long years to gain sophistication; twenty seconds to lose it all.

On the ride to the ballpark, Cody clearly wanted to continue his education. "But Dad, why do boys like girls?"

Hank had less than five minutes before he pulled into the parking lot. How could he do justice to this lofty topic in five minutes? He pasted on what he hoped looked like a fatherly expression. With a lot of luck, Cody wouldn't notice his dad's unease beneath his façade of nonchalance.

Cody grinned at his father, then stared out the truck window.

Cody's grin said it all. The kid knew just what his question did to his old man. He enjoyed watching his dad squirm.

Of course, Hank had done the same thing to his father. And his father had always answered all Hank's questions honestly, even the difficult ones. He just wished his father had been around with a few solutions that freshman year of college.

"You know how sometimes a girl makes you feel funny inside?"

"Like you want to do something silly to make her look at you?"

Hank kept his grin in check, barely. "Yeah, just like that."

Cody paused. Then he asked, "Did my momma make you feel that way?"

Hank tried to find the right tone, solemn but not bitter. "Yeah. She did."

Cody's grin turned into an accusatory stare. "But then things got in the way?"

Hank knew this day would come. How did he answer? "Sometimes, people don't understand what's important."

To Jennifer, leaving her problems behind had been important to her. She had wanted to pretend that her freshman year of college had never happened. She packed up and moved out of town as soon as the doctors released her. She couldn't be bothered to stick around to see if her baby survived his premature birth.

Instead she signed over all her parental rights with the stipulation that Hank never contact her. As far as Hank knew, she never looked back.

A bang on the outside of the truck door startled them both. B.J. jumped up and down outside the passenger window. "Come on, Cody. Let's warm up."

Hank whispered thanks for the reprieve. Someday he would have to finish this conversation, but not today. "After the game, do you want to rent a movie to watch since its B.J.'s turn to spend the night with us?"

Cody's bottom lip pooched. "I'm not sure he's still spending the night since his sister's home. He'll probably want to go home with her."

"Maybe we can convince her to watch the movie with us?" Maybe the boys would be so interested in the show that he could get Lacey alone on the front porch for a heart-to-heart.

And maybe pigs would fly.

Hank thought of all the dates his son had sabotaged. Everyone in town knew that Cody wasn't big on sharing his dad, especially with women. Hank had never realized why until today.

A smattering of cars squatted among the pick-ups in the parking lot, but none of them belonged to the Seivers. Hank pulled up next to a Chevy Silverado with the sticker still on the window.

"Looks like someone's got a new truck."

"Un-huh." Cody barely grunted out a reply. He climbed out of the truck to head for the ballfield, shutting the door harder than necessary to show Hank his opinion of inviting Lacey over.

Now that Hank understood Cody's resentment, grown-up friendship was another conversation Hank needed to have. He rubbed his hand over his eyes. Cody was growing up quicker than Hank could keep up.

Stalling to gather his composure, Hank took his time admiring the new truck parked next to his.

The Chevy was a fine looking truck, all decked out with running boards and leather seats. It even had a heavy-duty trailer hitch attached to the frame. Maybe in a couple of years, Hank could afford this truck—used.

He just hoped he could baby his old extended-cab Dodge long enough to get his plane motor paid for. But the transmission had been making a grinding noise and it wasn't shifting as tight as it should.

Still, the Dodge was his, bought and paid for. He

would give it a good wash tomorrow to apologize for wanting to trade it in.

Hank unloaded the equipment bag from the truck bed, remembering at the last minute to grab the two new bats from the gun rack behind his seat, while Cody ran ahead to the field. Three of his players' mothers perched on the bleachers just outside the dugout. The women wore matching shorts and shirts that said "I'm such and such's mom" on the back. Donna Sue Mabury was on the field throwing a ball to her husband, Richard. Richard's glove popped every time he caught the ball. Donna Sue could still zing them in.

Donna Sue had gone to LSU a few years before Hank on a softball scholarship. Unlike Hank, she had graduated. Now she played Sunday afternoon softball every chance she got to relieve the tension of being a divorce lawyer. Donna Sue probably knew more dirt on the good citizens of West Monroe than the whole Pilsner Street adult Sunday school class put together, but she kept secrets as well as a priest in a confessional. She certainly had a couple of his locked away.

With Zeb and Josh, his team would have eight players, almost a full team. For a parents' game, it was one of the bigger turnouts he'd had.

Nine- and ten-year-olds scrambled among the bleachers, yelling to each other as they discussed the line-up.

"Hank, could you help me? I'm not quite sure I remember how to hold this bat," Betty Chesterfield called to him from the batter's box. *How could a woman's voice sound so strident, yet so squeaky at the same time?*

"I'll be right there, Betty." Hank heard Zeb's truck before he saw it. It bounced to a stop and Josh, Zeb, and B.J. jumped out.

"We're gonna wi-in. We're gonna wi-in," B.J. sang as he raced into the dugout and deposited his armload of bats and balls at his coach's feet. "Where's Cody?"

Hank pointed to Cody, who was throwing a ball to Jana Griggs, mother of Winnie Griggs and one of the kindergarten teachers at Cody's grade school.

"Hey Cody, throw to me too." B.J. loped out to the field, displaying all the grace of a natural-born athlete, even at his age. Unlike Cody, B.J. rarely tripped over his own feet, but he always steadied his best friend when Cody stumbled. From experience, Hank knew that the boys wouldn't appreciate their friendship until they were older, just like he hadn't valued Lacey's.

Hank laughed at the relief glowing in Cody's eyes as B.J. joined him on the field. Cody hadn't relished playing catch with his old teacher Ms. Griggs since she shrieked every time she tried to catch the ball. Hank had been a bit surprised when Cody had volunteered to play catch with Winnie's mom. But then Winnie had joined them, and Hank had understood.

While Jana had struggled with putting on her glove, Cody had stood by hypnotized, as Winnie twirled a lock of hair around her finger. Someday, way too soon, that would be his little boy wrapped around some girl's little pinkie. How could he prepare Cody for the grown-up world, teach his son the ways of women, when he didn't understand them himself?

Hank and Jana had dated a few times, more out of
boredom than attraction. She was a classy lady. Hank
had been a little disappointed he couldn't work up any
enthusiasm for her.

Betty thumped her bat on home plate, broadcasting
her annoyance in having to wait for Hank to join her.

He plastered a good-mannered smile on his face and
headed for the batter's box, but stopped short when the
car he'd been watching for pulled into a parking place
behind the home team's dugout.

Glenna Seivers parked her car next to her son's truck
and climbed from the driver's seat. Hank saw Lacey
looking through the back seat window and felt too excited for his own good.

He flexed, lifting the bat above his head and ignored
Betty's impatient foot shuffling. Knowing Lacey would
cheer him on was nice, just like she used to do in high
school. Only this time, that skinny nerdboy, Mitch,
wouldn't be sitting next to her. Now, Mitch lived in
Silicon Valley and made his fortune designing computer
chips.

Billy went to the trunk and lifted out the equipment
bag, while Glenna waded through a throng of boys and
girls wanting her immediate attention.

And Lacey just sat there.

Through the back window of the car, Lacey watched
Hank walk to the batter's box. He wrapped his arms
around a big-busted woman who looked faintly familiar.
Together they swung the bat. Even from this distance,

his shoulders looked massive as they rotated through the move.

She worried her bottom lip between her teeth before she could stop herself.

Nothing had changed in the last ten years. A long time ago, Lacey had made peace with the knowledge that the girl on Hank's arm would never be her. Today it was an uneasy peace.

The ballpark looked the same as it did when Lacey last played. And it felt the same too. It felt like humiliation.

Among all the other klutzes and geeks on her mother's team, Lacey had been a below-average player. She knew, as did everyone else, that she couldn't hold an aluminum bat to the kids who were always picked for the champion teams.

"Lacey, are you all right?" Billy bent down to look into his daughter's face. "If you really don't want to do this, your mother will understand."

Lacey heard sympathy laced with challenge in his voice. Her father knew his daughter well. Pop was probably the only person in the whole world who knew how much Lacey dreaded this game. And he knew how much more she would dread not going through with it.

Billy probably wanted to play in this game as little as Lacey did, but he would cut off his right hand for his wife. And Lacey would repay her mother for all those years she had gathered together a flock of clumsy children and tried to convince them they played for the fun of it, not for the win.

Besides, nothing and no one would stand in Lacey

Seivers' way—not even herself with her almost paralyzing fear of embarrassment.

Lacey reapplied the lipstick she had eaten off, taking comfort in her coat of war paint. Breathing in courage along with the dust of the parking lot, she climbed from the back of her mother's car.

Self-consciously she tugged down her oversized T-shirt then trotted out to take her place next to Jana Griggs in outfield.

Jana had graduated high school three years before Lacey and Hank and went to college at ULM in Monroe to stay close to her family. She was probably the only girl in West Monroe who'd never spent time on the baseball diamond and didn't suffer the consequences of being labeled an outcast. She'd been inside the gym, swinging from the gymnastics bars instead, a feat that still made Lacey shiver.

"Hey Jana, I'm surprised to see you out here."

"Lacey? When did you get in?" Jana let a ball roll past her feet as she threw her glove on the ground and hugged her old friend.

"This afternoon." Lacey dropped her own glove to hug her back. Except for her family, this was her first welcome home. "I'd never expect to see you out here."

"You, either. The things we do for family." Jana blew her bangs off her forehead and shrugged.

"Head's up, sis. Here comes a pop fly." B.J. threw a ball high into the air, several feet short of Lacey, motivation enough for her to retrieve her glove.

"I'm ready, Beej. Fire it in here." Thankfully, B.J.

didn't take her seriously. Both boys politely rolled slow grounders to the women, showing great patience as Lacey and Jana missed each one. The whole time, Lacey felt the special prickle on the back of her neck that alerted her that Hank was nearby.

As Lacey chased after a ball that had dribbled past her glove, she glanced over her shoulder to see Hank watching her. Not looking where she was going, she ran past the ball and into the fence.

Finally the boys gave up trying to get the women to catch a ball and wondered off to climb on the bleachers.

Jana trailed Lacey into the dugout and took a seat on the scarred wooden bench. "Betty is something else. That's the third time she's drug Hank to the plate to show her how to hold that bat. Her flirting is getting a bit ridiculous."

As Lacey watched Hank show the well-endowed woman how to grip the aluminum bat, her stomach lurched, grumbling and gurgling. Not that Lacey was jealous or anything. That knot in her tummy was just pre-game jitters.

"I wish I could still fit into the clothes I wore in college." Jana startled Lacey out of her musings.

"There's no way Betty could fit into anything she wore back then."

"I wasn't talking about Betty." Jana stared at Hank. "He's wearing the same pants he wore at LSU, and they fit better now than they did then."

Of course Jana noticed the way Hank's baseball uniform fit. To look at Hank without an increase in pulse rate would be impossible for any red-blooded American woman.

The game progressed much as Lacey had been afraid of. With her brothers, Donna Sue, and Hank on one team and she, Jana, and Billy on the other, the game was lost before it was played.

She struck out twice, missed an easy pop fly, and tripped over a grounder that she tried to scoop up on the run. Although she'd kept the full width of the field between her and Hank, she'd felt as if he were breathing down her neck the whole time.

In reality, he treated her no differently than any of the other once-a-year players. He called encouragement when she found the ball hidden in the grass and cheered when she came up to bat just like he did for Jana and for Betty. Of course, his well-meant applause only made her screw up more often.

Her only consolation was that Jana played worse. But then, Jana didn't sweat.

"Come on, Lacey. The fat lady hasn't sung yet!" Jana called as Lacey walked to the plate, her bat on her shoulder.

Encouraged by the whoops and catcalls from her mom's team, she was determined to keep her eyes open during the pitch this time.

She swung at the first pitch and, amazingly, connected, sending a bouncing grounder toward second. Hank scooped up the ball and threw it but his first baseman bobbled the catch and the ball rolled to the ground.

"Yerrrrrrrr safe!" her mother called with overdone enthusiasm.

Dancing on top of the bag, Lacey beamed with victory.

"Come on, Pop. Hit a good one!" she yelled to her father.

He stepped up to the batter's box and scuffed the toe of his cowboy boot in the dirt.

"Put one over the fence, honey," his unbiased umpire-wife called.

He rubbed his hands dry on the backside of his jeans and winked at his wife, then turned to the pitcher. "Fire your best one at me, Donna Sue."

Lacey winced at her father's request. Surely, Donna Sue had sense enough to not take him at his word. Otherwise, Billy would be facing a fifty-mile-per-hour pitch.

Donna Sue wound up big and released the ball.

The bat cracked with an impressive sound, and Lacey took off for second base at a run.

She had only one choice. She would regret it in the morning, but she was not going to get tagged out. Lacey lunged for the bag, face first and came up sputtering dirt at Hank's feet.

Hank hauled her to her feet. She had jello for knees but she couldn't say if the unsteady wobble was from her daredevil play or because Hank's hands wrapped around her waist to steady her.

"Good slide, Lacey." The rumble of Hank's voice reverberated deep inside her.

Vaguely, she heard her mother make the call. "She's safe!"

"Momma! Hank got her by a mile! He tagged her be-fore she even got close to the base." At Josh's protest, Lacey blinked her world back into focus.

"Do you want to do your own laundry from now on?" Glenna asked in her biggest umpire voice.

Even a wooden bat could see that Glenna meant what she said.

"No, ma'am. She was safe." Defeated, Josh slumped his shoulders and kicked at the dust around second base.

Too aware of Hank's arms around her, supporting her, Lacey fought between pushing away to stand on her own two feet or giving into the desire to stay right where she was.

Suddenly, she had no choice. When Hank turned her loose and took away the warmth of his hands, Lacey felt like the sun had gone behind the clouds. She brushed her-self off as best she could but her filthy hands just made matters worse. Hopefully, her ankle wouldn't swell until after she reached the dugout.

"Missed her, missed her. Now you gotta kiss her!" B.J. yelled his singsong chant from the bench.

First one kid, then another, joined in until the whole team was hollering loud enough to hear in the next field. Donna Sue held the ball on the pitcher's mound, grinning and waiting.

Lacey's blood rushed to her face. In all her fan-tasies of kissing Hank, a crowded baseball field with bleachers full of nine-year-olds had never been the setting. Lacy wished the earth would crack open and swallow her.

Hank seemed as embarrassed as she was. He took off his hat and swiped the back of his hand across his forehead.

From right field, Betty yelled, "Play ball!"

Lacey stared at Betty flapping her arms to gain attention, but no one else seemed to have heard her.

Hank plopped his fist into his glove twice, cleared his throat, and resettled his hat.

The chant grew, picking up reinforcements from the Snack Shack behind the dugout. "Missed her, missed her. Now you gotta kiss her!"

"It's hot out here. Play ball!" Betty's voice reminded Lacey of a crow attacking a baby sparrow's nest.

An imp of an idea settled on Lacey's shoulder, startling her with a boldness she'd never had before.

Betty hadn't seen hot yet.

"Hank?" Lacey called in her most innocent voice.

"Yeah, Lacey?"

"I dare you."

Hank quirked an eyebrow. "You dare me?"

"I double dare you."

Chapter Four

Lacey licked her lips, hoping to tease a reaction from him.

Hank took the bait.

Just as he bent to reach her mouth, Lacey lost her nerve. She puckered up for a quick little kiss, ready to dodge away once the deed was done.

Obviously, Hank had other plans. He wrapped his arms around her and lifted her off her feet. Bending her over his arm in a move so smooth it made Patrick Swayze pale, Hank planted his lips on hers.

His warm mouth felt so luscious, Lacey had to have a taste. She parted her lips and ran her tongue across his bottom lip.

Hank groaned and buried his head in her neck. "Lacey, sweetheart. You've got to stop. You're killing me."

Heat flamed her face as she remembered her audience.

He lowered her feet to the ground but kept his arms around her. He must have known she wasn't ready to stand on her own yet.

As if waking from a dream, Lacey sifted through the fuzziness in her brain. Suddenly conscious of where her hands were, entwined in Hank's thick hair, she moved them to his shoulders instead. Whoops and whistles replaced the rush of her heartbeat in her ears.

"Oh, Hank. What have we done?" Lacey opened her eyes, then squeezed them shut again.

"You've never lacked for courage, Lacey. Now isn't the time to go chicken on me."

Lacey nodded her head and prepared to push away from the sanctuary of Hank's embrace. In one swift move, she unlatched from him and turned to give the cheering bleachers a sweeping bow.

Doffing her imaginary hat, Lacey bowed to the infield, then to the outfield.

Even from second base, Lacey saw Betty scowl from right field. She hadn't made a friend of Miss Betty today.

"Play ball," Betty cawed with her hands on her hips, glaring at Lacey.

Hank moved a few steps away and nodded to Donna Sue.

Lacey stood on second base, studiously watching the batter. She itched to look at Hank, to see what lasting effects this kiss had on him, but didn't trust herself to only give him a quick glimpse. What if her eyes froze on him and she couldn't even blink? Everyone would notice.

She had entertained the spectators enough for one day.

Lacey watched each pitch, begging the batter to hit one so she could get off this dratted field.

He crouched less than two arms' lengths away. Without looking, Lacey knew each time Hank shifted his weight. The back of her neck tingled and her palms sweated. Her lips felt swollen and itched like they needed to be touched.

Before she thought about it, she brushed her fingertip across her mouth and stole a sideways glance in Hank's direction.

His stare caught her and held her, sending messages that she couldn't interpret. His eyes, those deep-chocolate eyes, had darkened to onyx. She had never seen this expression on her friend's face before. No matter how hard she looked, she couldn't find the slightest trace of the comfortable best friend Hank had always been.

A knot the size of a softball settled low in her stomach. *You've really screwed up this time, Lacey.*

Time hung in Hank's stare.

"Ball game." The plate umpire released her from her second-base prison as the final batter struck out.

Lacey hustled to the dugout and scooped up her glove, then headed toward her mom's car, giving quick, tremulous smiles to those who wanted to make small talk.

Her brother Zeb followed her with the key. He opened his mouth to say something but Lacey would never know what that something was. The look on her face must have been enough to stop him.

He unlocked the door without a word before heading back toward the field.

Lacey sat in the back seat of the car and fought the mortification that threatened to swamp her.

The drive home was silent except for the radio. When they stopped for milk and eggs, Lacey wanted to hunch down low in the back seat so passersby couldn't see her, but her dignity had suffered enough already. Instead she stared out the side window and tried not to think about the whole incident.

But that kiss, that hot, tingling kiss, still burned on her lips.

If she were honest with herself, she'd have to admit that she'd forgotten about the crowd, forgotten about being just friends, forgotten her own name when Hank's mouth touched hers.

Pop pulled up to the house and parked next to Zeb's truck. "It's all right, baby girl. You're home safe now."

Glenna waited for Lacey to climb out of the car, then gave her a little hug. "A plate of brownies, a nice hot bath, and a good night's sleep will make all this look like fun in the morning."

Zeb and B.J. looked up from their TV show when she entered the living room. Fresh from the shower, Zeb's hair still sparkled with water. His neat, clean pleated khakis and polo shirt made Lacey feel even grungier in her filthy T-shirt. She heard the shower running and figured that Josh must be taking his turn.

Great, just great. For the hot water heater to catch back up would take at least a half hour.

B.J. bounced on the couch, knocking the afghan to the floor. "Wow, Lacey, I can't believe you kissed Cody's dad like that in front of everybody."

Zeb threw a pillow at his little brother. "Hush, B.J. We talked about not teasing Lacey."

"I wasn't teasing, I was just saying . . ."

Zeb narrowed his eyes at his little brother in warning. "Beej, leave it alone."

With a half-hearted shrug, B.J. turned his attention back to the TV show, but Lacey saw the covert glances he kept sneaking at her.

She sat next to him and put her arm around his shoulder. "It was a joke between two good friends that got out of hand. That's all. The less people say, the sooner the attention will die down."

Josh came out of his room, dressed for an evening out in his newest blue jeans and an ironed button-down shirt instead of one of his usual logo'd T-shirts. "Did you ask her?"

"Not yet." With concern written on his face, Zeb asked, "Lacey, do you want to go with Josh and me? We're meeting some friends, and you're welcome to come along." Although Zeb meant well, the kindness in his voice set Lacey's teeth on edge.

"No, thanks. I think I'll watch some TV, then take a long hot soak so I won't be too sore in the morning."

"That *was* a great slide, even though Hank tagged you out." Josh gave her a cautious grin.

Her brothers had never been this wary around her before. What did they expect? For her to burst out in tears?

Of course, the odds were fifty/fifty about now, but if they kept being so solicitous of her, she might not be able to hold back the flow.

She forced out her own smile. "I was safe. The umpire said so."

A phone call for B.J. interrupted their strained banter. Although B.J. tried to be discreet, Lacey easily overheard his stage whisper, "Hey Winnie, I'm not supposed to talk about it in front of Lacey. I'll call you back tomorrow."

Zeb and Josh each gave her a hug before they left, and Glenna put an extra dab of whipped cream on her plate of brownies. Her parents, B.J., and she munched in front of the TV, avoiding conversation.

Lacey was on her third piece, one more than her usual limit, when the local newsbreak flashed a video of the ballpark and the announcer said, "Tonight's 10-and-under season opener took on a new twist as spectators watched. More at ten o'clock."

Lacey choked as the brownie became a big wad of cotton in her mouth. Small-town news traveled way too far, way too fast.

"Do you think they mean Lacey and Hank, Pop?"

"I don't know, B.J. We'll have to watch and see. Do you need some water, Lacey?"

She waved away her father's offer and concentrated on her food. Finally, after some cautious chewing, she swallowed down the bite of brownie. "I think I'll take a bath now."

While she ran the water, Glenna brought Lacey a

bottle of her special bubble bath and her bath pillow, items that had always been reserved for chicken pox or the flu.

The long soak gave her time to think, time she'd rather not have had. Sure, she'd been embarrassed. No doubt, she'd hear a few snickers and remarks all week, but she could live with them. The way that kiss made her feel had her the most worried.

She might not have kissed dozens of men, but she'd kissed her share. None of them had come close to making her insides melt like Hank had. And he didn't even know it.

"Dad, why did you kiss Lacey like that?" Cody quit slurping on his cherry Icee long enough to pin his father to the dashboard with his stare.

"It was in fun, Cody. Just a silly thing to do. That's all."

At least that's how it had started. Finishing that kiss had taken a serious effort.

"Well, I didn't think it was very funny. All the guys ragged me about it until Zeb made them stop. I don't think *he* thought it was funny, either. And now B.J.'s not spending the night with me." Cody studied the inside of his plastic cup. "I don't think you should be kissing on girls, Dad. You're kinda old for it. And besides, you're my dad."

The kid might be right. But for a minute there, wrapped in Lacey's arms, Hank had felt more like a man than a father. And it was a pretty good feeling.

But it might be addictive and that wouldn't do at all.

Hank had a nine-year-old boy to raise. He didn't need the complications of a woman in his life.

What was he thinking? Lacey was his friend. That was all. Even if he did want something more, she wouldn't consider it. She had her career, her life, in Chicago. And he had his and his son's in West Monroe.

Hank's wayward imagination conjured up an image of Lacey meeting him at home after a long day at work. He'd rub her shoulders while she told him about her newest case. He would nod like he understood and patiently wait his turn to tell her about the cotton crop near Bee's Bayou. Then they would—

"Dad? Are we going somewhere? You missed the turnoff."

Sure enough, Hank had passed his own road by half a mile. He thought of some sort of excuse he could offer his son but couldn't come up with a thing. Instead he turned around in the next drive and headed back toward home.

As they passed the Seivers' house, Hank avoided looking in that direction. He'd likely run off the road if he saw Lacey.

Instead he hustled Cody inside with promises of another chapter of the newest Potter book after Cody showered.

As he listened to his pride and joy warble off-key under the showerhead, Hank wished his heart was as carefree as his son's. Instead, he'd been given the one gift he had never expected to get, Lacey's passionate kiss, and he didn't know what to do with it.

When Cody shut off the shower, the old pipes clanked and rattled. The noise gave Hank just enough heads-up time to gather his composure before Cody would track him down to continue the interrogation.

And Cody *would* grill him. The boy never let go of anything until he exhausted the topic, as well as the folks around him.

Hank swooped a clean dishrag across the kitchen table and popped open the dishwasher door. Over the rattle of dishes, he heard the bathroom door squeak open and footsteps pad down the hall.

"Dad, I've got a question about kissing." Cody didn't believe in pulling his punches.

Thankfully, Hank had practiced his mildly curious expression until it was almost natural. As shy as his son could be, any stronger emotion like shock or amusement or disapproval might make Cody hesitate to come to him. He never wanted to discourage his son from asking him questions, because Cody would find the answer by trial and error if not by asking his dad.

Hank would get this parenting thing right. "What's your question, son."

"When you want to kiss someone, what if you have stinky breath?"

Okay, this one wasn't as hard as it could have been. "If you brush your teeth, you won't have stinky breath."

"Does Lacey brush her teeth, Dad?"

Feeling like Cody had just sucker punched him, Hank tightened his stomach muscles too late.

He tried to block the memory of that kiss. He really

did. But the taste of Lacey sweetened his mouth even now.

Think, Hank, think. "Do you think B.J.'s mom would let any of her kids get away without brushing their teeth?"

Cody's brow furrowed as he pondered his dad's words. Glenna Seivers might be Cody's only example of motherhood, but she was also the best.

"You're right, Dad. That time we went camping in B.J.'s backyard, Ms. Glenna made us brush our teeth before we went outside."

You're right, Dad. Hank savored Cody's words. Funny how the little things kept you going. In this day of mixed victories, Hank clung to his one surefire success.

Hank pulled the ironing board from the closet, grimacing when it squealed as he unfolded it. "Now, go brush *your* teeth then hop in bed, and I'll be in to tuck you in when I get this shirt ironed."

Hank attacked the collar, grinding the iron into the hapless cotton to force it into proper shape. If only he could force his thoughts as easily.

Thoughts of marriage hadn't bothered him too much until recently. Not until he found his first gray hair the other day and realized he had no one to share it with.

Sometimes, late at night, he would convince himself that finding a nice woman to marry might be the best thing for Cody. But in the light of day, his sanity would return.

Hank *would* set a good example for Cody. Heaven

knew there were enough busybodies in town, under-mining his efforts by leaking tales of his wild teenage years to his big-eared son. Of course, the stories were always disguised as humorous childhood anecdotes.

Steam spewed, a reminder to keep the iron moving. Hank could do without an emergency run to Wal-Mart in the morning to replace a scorched shirt.

With the rising steam, a whiff of scent rose to tickle Hank's nose.

He sniffed at Cody's dress shirt. Nothing but detergent.

As he leaned over the ironing board, another blast of steam warmed his chest and he caught the scent again. He grabbed the front of his jersey and held it to his nose.

It must have happened when he had held Lacey so close. Her perfume had rubbed off on his shirt. Hank breathed deeply. The smell of Lacey intermingled with his own scent. The fragrance was headier than any formula a perfumer could bottle.

Lacey had felt so right, wrapped in his arms.

The iron belched a cloud of steam, curling the hairs on Hank's hand.

He had to get his mind off Lacey and onto more immediate problems. Like trying to get Cody's shirt ironed before he burned it.

Hank checked his own dress wear. His one good suit, a practical navy, had been worn only twice. The silk tie was new, burgundy with squiggles, but it still looked like a noose to him.

What would Lacey think of him all dressed up? He smoothed the tie, freeing it where it had become entangled with the coat hanger. She saw men in suits every day. He wouldn't look any different than the dozens of men she worked with—unless he started choking with that tie wrapped around his neck. That wasn't exactly how he wanted to be noticed.

Hank had to stop thinking about Lacey. He had an early morning and needed his sleep.

Hours later, his thoughts of Lacey turned to dreams of her—wonderful, exciting fantasies that her father would shoot him for if Billy knew what Hank had dreamed.

Emerging from his shower, a cooler one than usual, Hank hit the alarm as it began its first screech.

The moon faded into the pale morning sky, reminding Hank that his dreams were made of no stronger stuff than moonlight. And like the moon, they would have to be hidden in the light of day.

After a restless night, Lacey flung herself from her bed. How could she have done something so stupid? That dumb dare and the public exhibition that followed was so bad that her brothers hadn't even picked on her about it.

Of course, Lacey was grateful for Zeb's help but she must be in really deep do-do to have the world's biggest teaser refrain from his usual jokes.

For a split second, she thought about burrowing deep

under her sheets and staying there until her vacation ended.

No! She would *not* spend her treasured vacation days hiding out. Pushing back the covers, she stretched, realizing every muscle protested. Yesterday's slide had been daring at the time. Now, it seemed foolish.

But then that whole ball game had turned into a big humiliating joke.

Deliberately she pushed yesterday behind her, determined to enjoy the here-and-now.

Sunbeams shined through a crack in the pink curtains and warmed her face. She breathed in the scent of her room. The baby powder, trapped in the cracks between the oak planks, was the smell she missed the most.

She sat up, pushed her mussed hair behind her ears and twisted her gym shorts straight around her waist. A draft swept under her oversized T-shirt, encouraging her to scoot back under the covers. Instead, she blinked her sleep-deprived eyes and absorbed the tranquility of being home along with the familiar sight of her teen-decorated room.

Over her twin-sized bed, she'd hung her Patrick Swayze poster so he would be the last thing she saw before she went to sleep. The scrape marks on the wooden planks showed where she had pushed all her furniture against the doors to keep out her brothers. Nesting under her covers lay her stuffed purple bunny. Hank, Zeb, and Josh had pooled their lunch money and bought Mr. Burple for her sixth-grade graduation.

She hugged the threadbare rabbit and hunted for the tack holes in the ceiling that had held Patrick captive.

Her room was so different from her apartment. Just like she was so different from the girl who used to live here.

Lacey lay on her stomach and slid her head toward the floorboards. She reached for her cardboard treasure chest, an old shoebox, just beyond her fingertips.

"Hey, Lacey. Whatcha doing upside down?" B.J. grinned from her doorway, then bounced into the room and bent over to look under her bed with her. "You trying to reach that box? I'll get it." He dragged it out and set it on her bed. When he plopped next to his sister the box tipped, spilling pictures all over her bedspread.

Lacey studied a yellowing dog-eared one. Six-year-old Hank smiled at her, his missing front tooth obvious. Carefully, Lacey laid the old photo back in the box. Then she pulled out a plastic card, Hank's first driver's license. Only Hank could get a decent picture from the DMV mugshot cameras.

B.J. rifled through her treasures, studying one and then the next. "These are mostly pictures of Hank. Look at this one with this pretty girl. He's got two pictures of you next to his bed, but I bet he doesn't have this many."

"Hank's got pictures of me? Which ones?"

"One with you holding a certificate and another with you hugging on him. He's got pictures of Cody and me on Cody's nightstand, too. He says that it's good to have your best friends close sometimes."

Best friends. That about summed it up. She and Hank were best friends, just like B.J. and Cody. Surely if she gave him a good, hard, critical look, she'd come to realize that the man was just flesh and blood.

Oh, but what flesh he was! And he certainly made her blood run hot.

"What's wrong, Lacey? Your face just turned red." B.J. dug through the box for another photo.

What's wrong was that Lacey still had a bad teenage crush on her best friend. "Just wayward thoughts. Nothing important."

She *would* rid herself of this silly infatuation before the week was out.

"Look at this one, Lacey." B.J. stuck a brittle newspaper clipping under her nose. "It says 'Hank Chandler, Louisiana's Top Recruit Will Call LSU's Dugout Home.' Here's a picture of the president of LSU shaking Hank's hand. Wait'll I tell Cody."

"Be careful with that, Beej. It looks like it's ready to crumble." Lacey rescued the clipping and studied the grainy photo. As usual, girls flanked Hank, with Jennifer vying for prime position.

How much had Hank told his son about Jennifer? Everyone in West Monroe whispered and speculated, but Hank had never confirmed nor denied. With Cody getting older, the boy was bound to be curious about who his mother is. And little boys usually found what they were looking for, even if they didn't always look in the best places.

"B.J.? Are you in there?" Glenna peeped into the

room. "Your father is ready to call out your spelling words before he runs into town."

With dragging feet, B.J. slunk toward the bedroom door. "Can we look at more pictures later, Lacey?"

"Sure, B.J. Why don't we dig out your baby pictures next? You were such a cute baby." Lacey winked at her mom as Glenna stood, hands on hips, waiting for her son.

"Yeah. That would be cool. Was I cuter than Josh and Zeb, Momma?"

Lacey didn't catch Glenna's reply, as mother and son left her room. No doubt, it was the perfect, diplomatic answer to B.J.'s baited question. When the time came, Lacey hoped she had half her mother's savvy for raising children.

Of course, that time seemed to slip further away every second.

Lacey scooped up a handful of pennies that had fallen out of her photo box. She dropped them in the plaster cow bank that sat on her dresser. How many dimes and quarters had she hoarded so carefully in that turquoise cow? The change that jingled in her cow bank made a meager jangle compared to the bottom figure in her checkbook.

Who would have ever guessed that Lacey Seivers of West Monroe, Louisiana, always the last one picked for dodge ball, would have a big time career as a corporate lawyer, complete with a window view and an ergonomically correct chair?

And the next rung of her "ladder of success" was within reach. If—no—when, the senior partners agreed to give her the Alexander project, Lacey would be made junior partner. Along with the big pay raise would come an office with a door and a team of assistants that she could hand pick.

What she needed was some nice, safe, ordinary work to keep her mind off her ludicrous fantasies of Hank and that kiss. A morning immersed in company email should set her back to normal in no time.

She set up her laptop on the footstool in the den and settled on the rug to reconnect with Chicago and reality. The rural phone connection was a lot slower than her intracompany network, but it finally pulled up her email messages.

Halfway down the screen she spotted a message that instantly changed her worries from home life to work life. Kelly, the smartest paralegal Lacey had ever met, kept Lacey caught up on the undercurrents from the seniors' section. The subject header read "LACEY: Open Immediately."

She tapped her foot, waiting for the message to open.

Rumors are flying that Ted wants your case. He was spotted at the Tower Club having drinks with Mr. A. after work yesterday. Word has gotten out that this assignment is a stepping stone to bigger, better. You might want to cut that vacation short. K.

Too late, Lacey realized she'd just bitten off a nail.

"Lacey, you're up early." Billy stopped short of the front door and stepped toward his daughter instead.

"Good morning, Pop."

"Not so good from the sound of your voice." Billy sat

down behind his daughter and started to rub her shoulders. "Sweetie, I know you're upset about yesterday at the ballpark. But everyone there saw it as good fun. Nothing more. I've got a feeling it meant more to you than that, but nobody knows that except family." He brushed her hair from her face. "The longer you avoid Hank, the harder it will be to feel comfortable around him."

Pop understood her better than anyone else in the world. She hugged him, accepting the temporary protection of his strong arms.

After a few seconds, she found the strength to push away from his embrace.

"You're right, Pop. Hank's too good of a friend to lose because I'm too embarrassed to face him."

"Why don't you march right over there and say hello?"

"I think I will, right after I shower." Lacey looked down at her sleep shirt, already trying to decide what to wear to make the right impression.

Hot water didn't wash away her worries about Hank or her job. Blinking through the evaporating steam, Lacey stood in front of the mirror and ripped the rubber band from her ponytail. Winding the ends of her board-straight hair around the curling iron, she mocked herself for her indecision. It was just a walk down the road, a little stroll she had made a thousand times before.

She fluffed her curls, watching them return to their original, uncurled state.

Picking a cotton candy pink tank top, she layered it over a white tank. Her blue jean shorts would do.

Sandals would look better but she opted for tennies and white socks instead to keep the weeds and burs from scratching and the chiggers from biting. Some things a girl never forgot.

Drawing in a deep breath for courage, Lacey declared herself ready to face Hank. She resisted the urge to check the mirror one more time. Instead, she stomped from the room and out of the house, letting the screen door slam behind her.

And strutted herself straight to her father's shop for another pep talk.

"Hey, Pop, you got anything I need to take to Hank's?"

He straightened from his workbench and grinned. "I imagine I can find something around here that needs to be over there." He rooted through a box of parts and came up with a tire pressure gauge.

"Here you go. Tell Hank that I noticed his back left tire looked a little low."

Lacey stared at the tire gauge. "I'm being pretty silly about this, aren't I?"

Her pop shrugged his shoulders. "Love, in any form, has its challenges, baby girl. Whether it's family or friends or that special love between a man and a woman. And sometimes, it's not easy."

"Hank and I are just friends. That's all we've ever been, all we'll ever be."

"Ever is a long time." He bit down on his sucker and stared up at The Duke then back at his daughter. "I've always been proud of you for facing life straight-on."

"And you'll be even prouder when I take this tire gauge over to Hank, right?"

"That's right, baby girl."

"Then I better get going." With a wink and a cheeky grin, she saluted The Duke. "Daylight's burning, pilgrim."

As expected, Billy winced as she butchered his favorite John Wayne expression. He wound up the shop rag and popped it in her direction. "Then head 'em up and move 'em out, little doggie."

Lacey strolled down the road toward Hank's house, alternately humming and chewing on her bottom lip. She owed it to Hank and to herself to be honest about how she felt.

Well, not too honest. What would her best buddy do if she told him she'd wanted him since her teens? No, she wasn't willing to risk rejection, didn't want to see pity in his big brown eyes. But she would be honest about that kiss. Tell him that it had curled her toenails. Tell him she wanted another.

No, she should probably only tell him that she wanted to strengthen their friendship. And maybe, eventually, he'd want more than best buddy status too.

Today was too soon to think about long distance relationships. Still, she indulged in daydreams of walks together along Chicago's lakefront, exploring the museums, cuddling in front of her apartment's fireplace as the first snowfall of winter drifted in.

Deep, baritone laughter, followed by nine-year-old cackling brought her back to the warmth of May. And the sight of Hank in a wet white T-shirt made her morning even hotter.

Cody pointed the hose at his dad and released the kink he'd squeezed into it, spraying Hank from top to bottom.

"I got you good, Dad." Cody doubled over with laughter at his successful hit, too busy preening to notice that Hank had picked up the bucket of sudsy water.

"Yeah, you did, Cody, but you forgot the soap." Hank upended the bucket on his chortling son.

Cody held up his hands against the flow of water. The hose fell, squirting Cody as it wriggled to the ground. Through his giggles, Cody choked out, "You know what this means, don't you, Dad?"

Hank laughed, feeling the joy of childhood through his son. "I'm afraid so."

The hose lay on the freshly cut grass, squirming like a snake and creating rivers in the dry yard. Father and son eyed the hose, then each other.

Cody called the count. "On your mark. Get set. Go!"

They took off running for the hose, with Cody snatching it from his dad's hesitating hand. Hank let Cody spray him until he felt waterlogged. Then he tackled his son, rolling the two of them in the wet grass.

"Do you give?" Hank already knew the answer, but the pattern had been set since the time Cody could talk.

"Never."

"Never?" Hank tickled his son, while Cody tried to reach Hank's own ribs. Cody tugged at Hank's wrists until Hank gave in gracefully and allowed his son to pin his hands above his head.

"Now, Dad. Do *you* give?" Cody blinked through wet glasses, and a grin split his face.

Pride welled up in Hank. Pride and joy. Cody added so much to his life. Hank couldn't begin to imagine the hole that would be in his heart if anything ever happened to Cody. "I give, son. You win."

Cody crawled from the ground, his knee accidentally sinking into Hank's stomach. Hank bit back his grunt. The boy was as awkward as a puppy and so sensitive about it.

Wet grass covered Cody from head to toe. He scratched at the itchy grass before pulling off his shirt. Then he grabbed the hose and handed it to Hank. "Here Dad, squirt me off, then I'll squirt you."

Obligingly, Hank washed away the prickling grass blades. Then he peeled off his own cold, wet shirt and welcomed the morning sun's warmth on his bare skin.

"Oh, hi." Cody waved past Hank. "Where's B.J.?"

"He's playing video games," Lacey called from the end of the driveway.

Lacey? Lacey was here? Hearing her voice made Hank painfully conscious of how he was dressed. Or not dressed.

There he stood in soaked gym shorts. His big toe stuck through a hole in his deck shoes. Wet hair scraggled into his eyes.

He rubbed his hand across his face. Good gravy, he hadn't even shaved yet.

Chapter Five

Good gravy! The man looked good enough to eat! Lacey felt her blood pressure rise. There Hank stood, looking better than any pin-up she'd ever had the privilege of gawking at. Dark stubble outlined his jaw. His shoulders rippled as he pushed wet hair from his eyes. Water glistened on the tips of his eyelashes.

Lacey watched, entranced, as one intrepid drop escaped from a strand of chocolate-brown hair to run across Hank's cheek. The waterdrop dripped onto his muscled chest. Then the droplet gathered speed and joined the rivulet on its journey down Hank's washboard stomach, to pool in his flat belly button.

Lacey jerked her stare from the waterdrop's excursion and forced herself to look into Hank's face.

By his surprised expression—really more aghast than surprised—Lacey knew she had screwed up again.

Her fist tightened, biting into the tire pressure gauge. The tire pressure gauge! Her excuse for being here.

She uncramped her fingers, one by one, until she had her hand open. The gauge lay in her palm like a lifeline.

"Pop noticed your tire seemed to be low yesterday. He sent this to you." She thrust the little tool out to him as if it were a snake she was giving away.

Hank grinned and cocked an eyebrow. "Thanks. Billy must think I lost mine, huh?"

He brushed his fingers over her palm, making gelatin of her knees. Lacey leaned against his truck bumper for support. She tried to look nonchalant, but the trailer hitch made for an uncomfortable perch.

"I don't usually get a sunshiny day off this time of year, only the rainy ones that are too bad to fly in. But I had blocked off this afternoon for the graduation and when we had a cancellation this morning, I asked Glenna not to fill it. With the whole day off, Cody and I thought we would wash the truck this morning." Hank brushed at a drop of water as it trickled down his stomach.

Cody stared at Lacey, his forehead wrinkled in puzzlement. Pushing his glasses up on his nose, he studied Hank, then narrowed his eyes back at Lacey until she squirmed and looked away.

Hank shoved the gauge into his son's hand. "Check those tires for me, okay?"

Cody squatted to the closest tire. "This one's okay. Which tire did Mr. Seivers say needed air?"

Hank kept Lacey pinned with his gaze. "Check them all, son. I'm going in to get a clean shirt."

When Hank started toward the door, he released Lacey from his hypnotic stare. Finally, reprieve.

"Aren't you coming, Lacey?"

Lacey concentrated, trying to form a mental picture of John Wayne wading into the breach, waving his men forward. Finding strength in The Duke's image, she said under her breath, "Wagons ho."

"What's that?"

"Nothing. Just talking to myself."

While Hank disappeared into his bedroom, Lacey sat on the couch in the den and fidgeted for about half a second. The same couch and rocker sat in the same place they'd occupied for twenty years. But the big leather recliner was new. So was the entertainment center. And the mahogany piecrust serving table in the corner held more picture frames than she remembered.

Lacey picked up Rob's family picture, trying to find the resemblance between him and Hank. Rob was leaner, lankier, brown hair and eyes, but softer, more like topaz than dark chocolate. But that squared-off, stubborn jaw was both a physical trait and a personality trait he shared with his younger brother.

Lacey remembered the misery Hank had put Rob through after their father's death. Rob had only been nineteen then, just five years older than Hank. Still, he'd taken on the responsibility of trying to get Hank safely through his teenage years.

But Hank, angry over his father's death, had resented Rob's efforts, accusing him of trying to take their father's place. Then he'd set out to prove that Rob could never fill in for his father. Although he'd never been arrested, he'd seen the back seat of a patrol car more then once and the Ouachita Parish sheriff's department knew the way to Hank's house.

She and Rob had never been close, but once, just before she and Hank graduated high school, Rob had spotted her alone in the Dairy Queen and bought her a strawberry shake.

With a catch in his voice, he'd told her how grateful he and his mother were that Lacey was always there when Hank needed her. She was the only one Hank had ever really talked to. Without her friendship, Rob thought Hank might have self-destructed after their father's death. She was Hank's reality when all the other girls treated him as a superstar.

After he left, Lacey threw away the unfinished shake, drove to the empty ballpark, and cried all those tears Hank had never let fall.

Then she'd called him up for a movie, but he already had a date, so she'd mailed her college application to Notre Dame instead.

Hank had come so far. He owned his own plane; he owned a partnership in a solid business; and he raised his son with love. He was a man any father would be proud of.

Next to Rob's photo sat scores of Cody's pictures. From months-old infant to fifth grader, Cody smiled from the frames. He had the Chandler jaw, with Hank's dimple to soften it. But that pale blond hair and those crystal blue eyes were from his mother.

One photo, front and center, had a cardboard frame, decorated in glitter. In a child's hand, crooked crayoned words chased around the homemade square. "Happy Mother's Day to the best Dad in the world." A young Cody grinned with snaggle-toothed glee from his father's arms.

For just a second, Lacey imagined herself included in that picture.

Her heart filled with an emotion so overpowering she fought to define it. Sympathy for a boy with no mother? For a man raising his son alone? Joy in a father and son's closeness?

The answer blazed through her like a lightning bolt. The emotion was longing and it was all hers. Lacey picked up the photo for a better look. She would give anything to be part of this little family.

Lacey set the picture back in place and glanced around to see who had witnessed her revelation. Carefully, she willed her legs to carry her back to the couch where she sat before her knees gave out.

She was in love.

Not just infatuated, not just in awe of his male beauty. But totally, completely, absolutely in love with a soul that called out to him, a soul that couldn't fathom living without him.

A noise in the hall alerted her to Hank's return. His worn boots made a cadence on the wooden floor that beat in counterpoint to Lacey's heart. His face was smooth and he smelled of a cologne that he had made distinctly his own. Through love-clouded eyes, she saw more than a gorgeous body. She saw Hank, the man she wanted to grow old with.

"I want to talk about yesterday, Lacey." Hank took the chair opposite her and leaned forward, elbows on knees. "I want to talk about that kiss."

Dumbly, Lacey nodded her head.

"I'm sorry. I should have never done that." Hank scrubbed his hands through his hair and looked everywhere but at Lacey. "It was a foolish thing to do and it got a little out of hand. I should have remembered how you hated public scenes. Embarrassing you like that was thoughtless. I wish I could take it back, but I can't. Forgive me?"

All Lacey's illusions of home and hearth burst into flames. Ashes filled her heart and her mouth. She forced her lips to turn up in the corners.

"Well, it was fun while it lasted." She glanced at the clock on the wall without seeing the hands. "I've got to get back home. I've got lots to do before the graduation this afternoon."

Hank stood and walked her to the door. "Thanks for bringing the tire gauge."

Lacey tripped on the bottom step. Hank reached out and caught her arm to steady her. His touched burned so she turned to break the contact. Her impulsive action put them chest-to-chest, just like last night. She jerked her arm away and took a step back.

Lacey spoke to his boots. "See you later, Hank." She coughed to disguise the strangled sound of her voice.

The walk home seemed to take forever. Over and over she played Hank's words in her head. 'It should have never happened. I wish I could take it back, but I can't.'

That's what he had said the night he called to say he was proposing to Jennifer all those years ago. She knew where she ranked now.

Once inside the safety of her home, Lacey curled up on the couch in the den with the portable phone, determined to make that call to the airlines. She had her career waiting for her in Chicago—a career that needed her time and attention, a career that she was darned good at and that gave her great satisfaction. To stay on the fast track would take all her waking hours and total focus.

Long distance friendship with Hank would be for the best for everybody. Besides, that's all she would ever get.

She punched in two dozen numbers, then absently listened to the recorded message requesting that she hold.

Being held captive by the calling queue gave her too much idle time to think. She had no one to blame but herself. Hank had never given any indication that they were more than friends.

Besides she had never been his type. The woman for Hank would have gloried in the attention at the ball field. His ideal mate would have swooped the crowd a bow that would have sent them all cheering. Okay, she had done that. Score two points. But her grand gesture had been spawned from desperation, not because she reveled in the attention.

In her ear, the giddy tune of "Tijuana Taxi" played through for the third time. She pulled her thoughts away from Hank by forcing herself to outline her schedule. She would sit through the graduation ceremony this afternoon, spend time tonight visiting with the folks, then take the first flight out tomorrow morning. That would give her a few hours in the office on Sunday afternoon to plan her counterdefense to Ted's attempt to steal her case from her.

"Hey, sis. Guess what?" B.J. shattered the monotonous mood of the phone music. "Mom says that Monday, you can coach third base for us! It's our first game of the season, and you've never seen me play. She says I'm at least as good as you were, and last year I hit one that rolled to the fence."

Lacey looked into B.J.'s bright face and hoped he was a lot better ballplayer than she ever was.

He saw the phone and whispered, "Oh, sorry," then made himself comfortable next to Lacey on the couch.

"It's okay. I'm on hold."

"Then I can tell you the other stuff Mom said we could do! Tuesday, when Mom goes to play Pokeno, you and me and Pop can cook hamburgers outside like he used to do when you were little. And Mom's gonna make that cake you like, the one with seven layers of icing. Even though it's a school night Tuesday, Mom said we could go to a movie together. And Wednesday . . . Why'd you hang up the phone?"

"The call wasn't that important." Lacey hugged her little brother, soaking in his warmth and enthusiasm. "Now, tell me about Wednesday."

"It chokes, Dad. Why do we have to wear these stupid things anyway?"

Hank loosened the knot on Cody's cartoon character tie then ruffled his son's hair. "I've often wondered that myself."

"I'll bet I know. It's 'cause ladies have to wear bras all the time, so they make us pay for it by making us wear ties."

"You know, Cody, in a million years I'd never have thought of that." He gave Cody a hug then tugged at his own burgundy silk tie. "I think you may be right, though."

Father and son peered into the tiny bathroom mirror. Cody worried that his friends would giggle at him all dressed up. Hank worried that Lacey might do the same thing—if she even bothered to glance his way.

He was having the hardest time figuring out if he was talking to a grown, sophisticated woman or if he was talking to his best friend. He was having an even harder time merging the two together. The old Lacey would have laughed off both the apology and the kiss. Well, maybe not the kiss. At least, he hoped she wouldn't have laughed about his kiss.

But wasn't that what he wanted? To have his best buddy back?

Now he was getting confused.

He couldn't predict what this new Lacey would do.

That tight little smile she had given him had been one hundred percent offended female.

He had thought he was doing the noble thing by apologizing, until Lacey had stared at him with that plastic smile.

He knew better. He knew the top item in the book of "what guys never say to a woman" was never apologize for a kiss. If he could only replay that scene over again, but he'd learned a long time ago that "do-overs" didn't happen.

Now how did he make it better?

He ran a comb through his son's hair one last time, pushing those too-long bangs from Cody's eyes. "Ready?"

"Sure, Dad." Cody looked very grown-up in his suit and tie. But he would always be Hank's little boy, that baby who grinned and burbled whenever he saw his bottle, or smiled so sweetly as he blew bubbles in his sleep, or still sought the occasional snuggle in his Dad's lap on cold, stormy nights.

Hank would have never believed he could have loved someone as much as he loved his son.

"Did you remember the colored pencils and the new comic book, Dad?"

Hank snagged his jacket from the back of the kitchen chair and patted the pockets. "Right here, Cody."

Cody squared his shoulders as if he were about to face a firing squad. "Then I guess we're ready." He let the screen door slam behind him. "We did a good job of cleaning your truck, didn't we, Dad?"

"Yes, we did." Had it only been this morning? Hank's day read like an emotional weather forecast. Grins and giggles in the morning, guilt and confusion by mid-afternoon.

Maybe he should send flowers? Or candy? Or maybe he'd read too much in Lacey's face and she wasn't as upset as he thought. After all, they were best friends, not lovers.

He had as much chance of becoming more than friends as he did of winning the lottery.

What he wanted to do was ask Billy's advice, but asking about how to make up to Billy's only daughter just didn't feel right, especially with Lacey starring in his nighttime fantasies.

As soon as Hank cranked up the truck, the radio blared out Shania Twain singing about "who's lips have you been kissing."

Cody pinned Hank with an accusatory stare. "We all know whose lips you've been kissing, Dad. And I don't think B.J.'s sister thought it was just for fun, either. I think she liked it—too much."

"Well, Cody, that would make two of us. I liked it too." There. Hank admitted it, not only to Cody but also to himself. When his lips locked onto Lacey's, he hadn't been kissing his ole' fishing buddy. He'd been kissing a full-grown woman who was also his best friend. And he had liked it immensely.

He caught himself whistling as Shania asked "who do you run to?" The answer was Lacey. And tonight he would apologize for apologizing and make it all better. He'd grovel if he had to. Their friendship was worth it.

He sure would like to try another kiss, too, but that seemed unlikely as well as unwise.

Cody wrapped his tie around his finger, scowling at the road in front of him.

Hank studied his son, his lonely only, who definitely resented sharing his dad. "You *will* be polite to Lacey, whether I kiss her again or not."

Cody glared out the window, his bottom lip poked out.

Hank assumed his most parental expression. "Did I hear you say 'yes, sir?' "

"Yes, sir."

Hank nodded in acceptance of Cody's mumbled reply. Only slightly content with his son's compliance, he drove the rest of the way in silence.

The boy was getting too old to be so possessive of his old man. His son would just have to get used to seeing his father happy in someone's company other than his own.

She would be gone in a week and everything would be back to normal.

He was happy with his life, wasn't he? He had his business, he could fly whenever he wanted to, his son was healthy and growing up just fine. What man could ask for more?

Since when did his pleasant little picture of his life

have a hole in it? And why was he so sure it was a Lacey-sized hole?

Once in the auditorium, Hank scanned the crowd for the Seivers family.

"There they are, Dad. Two sections down from the letter M." He saw four distinct blobs: Billy, Glenna, Lacey, and B. J.

Cody waved high over his head, and B.J. waved in return. "Can I go ahead?"

"Sure, son. Just don't run over anyone."

As Cody bounded up the stairs, Hank blinked to better focus. It appeared that woman was back, the one that had stolen Lacey and substituted a model in her place. Hank didn't know if he was more pleased or more intimidated.

He'd never been afraid of a woman in his life. This was Lacey after all. She might be all dressed up but she was still his best buddy under that classy blue dress.

Lacey stood up to let him scoot past her. He twisted and contorted but couldn't prevent a single touch with the back of his hand along her back. The touch was solely to guide her to her seat, he told himself.

His brain might say it, but his body didn't have to believe it. His fingers tingled, sending vibrations all the way to his toes.

He took the empty seat next to her and tried to squeeze his frame into the narrow folding chair.

"Nice, but a bit crooked." She reached out and straightened his tie.

He wanted to cover her hands with his own. Instead he clasped his fingers together into a tight fist and rested them in his lap.

"Thanks. You too." He tried not to, but couldn't help but notice how much Lacey had changed from that insecure high school girl she had been. Back then she never would have worn a dress as sophisticated as this one, not with such grace and elegance anyway.

The V-neck dipped down so that he could see the delicate silver chain with a pearl pendant dangling from it. It was the kind of necklace a man would give to a woman as a gift. An unreasonable jealousy rushed through him.

Hank slowly let out his own breath and made himself think beyond gifts of jewelry. Instead, he closed his eyes and tried to summon up an image of his best buddy in overalls with a smudge of dirt on her nose.

A bead of sweat rolled down his neck into his too-tight collar.

Just friends, just friends, just friends, just friends. Maybe if he kept up his silent chant, he'd make it through the next three hours, but he sure wouldn't bet on it.

Chapter Six

This graduation ceremony had to be the longest one in history. Three hours under normal circumstances would have been a trial, but sitting next to Lacey, smelling her perfume, updating all his memories of that cute little girl with this sensuous woman had nearly driven him mad.

The drive to the Warehouse with two wiggling, chatty boys in tow gave Hank a chance to regain his composure.

He made sure that he sat across from Lacey, not next to her, but still had trouble concentrating on the menu.

Get a hold of yourself, Hank. You're not eighteen anymore.

"Hey, Dad. I want a hamburger and fries but they only have them on the kid's menu and I don't want a kiddie meal."

93

Hank winked at the waitress. "My son will have one adult hamburger, no onions, no lettuce with an adult order of fries, please."

"Of course, sir. And what does his father want?"

"Steak, medium rare."

"What would you like on your potato?"

"Uh, I'd like fries too."

Josh grinned and elbowed him. "We certainly know where Cody gets his good taste from, don't we?"

"And to drink?"

"Tea, sweet, no lemon."

Sweet tea and a good steak. That's what Hank needed to set himself right. Outside the restaurant, the Ouachita River rolled past. Moonlight glimmered on the inky water, sending waves of peace through Hank.

Lacey ordered fried catfish and asked for extra ketchup for her fries. At least they still had French fried potatoes in common.

As the Seivers ordered food, exchanged banter, and toasted each other, Hank leaned back in his chair and relaxed. Affection freely shared washed over him. He would never be able to express his gratitude that Cody was growing up surrounded by this tight-knit love.

With Billy at one end of the table and Glenna at the other, Hank could almost forget that he wasn't really a part of this family.

But what he felt for Lacey wasn't the least bit brotherly, no matter how hard he tried. When Lacey laughed, her eyes sparkling and her mouth so soft, so kissable, he almost forgot he resolved to be just friends.

True to Saturday night small-town custom, every ten minutes or so someone would wander up for a tableside chat and he'd be reminded that Lacey was just here for a visit and she would soon be returning to Chicago.

He wished they'd all mind their own business and leave her alone. While he enjoyed chewing the fat as well as the next guy, he didn't like the way some of these visitors made Lacey squirm.

Most of the folks had sense enough to avoid any mention of the ballpark kiss. But they all commented about how she didn't look like she had in high school and how they would never have imagined that timid little Lacey would become a big city lawyer and the comparisons weren't always kind.

He had never given Lacey's teenage years much thought before. Looking back, he realized that she might not have had the flash and dash of a pin-up bikini babe, but she had been pretty, in a shy, quiet kind of way. And anyone who didn't know that she had always been as smart as a whip was an idiot.

For the first time ever, Hank realized why Lacey had moved away. How else could she have broken the unyielding stereotype of geeky mouse that this town had stamped her with? And with that understanding, he silently forgave her for deserting him, an offense he didn't even know he held against her until now.

"Lacey, is it really you? My goodness, I barely recognized you." Candice's high-pitched squeal made Hank grind his teeth. She hovered behind his chair, so close she made the hairs on the back of his neck raise. "Just look at you now. I'll bet you're making up for all the time you spent studying instead of dating in high school."

But Lacey, with a graciousness she inherited from Glenna, forced out a polite, slightly tight-lipped smile. "Hello, Candice. You're looking well, too."

"You know, Heather and I are still the best of friends and she told me that you only bought one ticket for the reunion ball. I'm on the registration committee. If you want, I can contact one of the guys who bought one ticket too and see if they would take you."

"No, thank you, Candice." Lacey didn't bother with a smile this time.

Candice must have figured out that she'd gone too far, because she turned her attention to Hank. "You haven't registered for the dance yet, Hank. It's five dollars higher at the door."

"I don't plan on going."

"Oh?" Candice darted a look at Cody then back to Hank. "Did you know that Jennifer Myers is coming to the dance? Imagine that, a Dallas Cowboys cheerleader from our very own graduating class returning to her hometown."

Jennifer? Here? Hank felt like a man being ripped from his own skin.

He gripped his chair, trying to hold onto a world out of his control, but his fingers felt numb and useless.

With no help from him, the whole Seivers family tried to redirect the conversation without seeming too obvious to Cody. He watched himself twirl his tea glass around keeping his attention on an individual drop of condensation trickling down the side.

And he could see his son, full attention turned to Candice, trying to figure out why their idyllic supper had turned into a nerve-snapping game of verbal dodge ball.

"C'mon, Hank." Lacey wedged between Candice and Hank's chair, then backed up, forcing distance between them. "You promised to take me siteseeing since Cody's spending the night with B.J."

He sat, unable to move, much less comprehend. But then Lacey laid her hand on his shoulder. As if she passed courage and strength from her body to his, he felt his mind refocus. When he scraped back his chair, the screeching rasped down his spine. He stood, bumping into Zeb, and threw some bills on the table to cover his and Cody's meal. Then he followed where she led, her slender fingers on his elbow, guiding him to safety.

Lacey's heart broke for Hank. For the next ten miles, they drove in silence. They ended up at The Point, his truck rocking down the rutted path to the sandy beach at the turn in the river.

With the motor off and the windows rolled down,

Lacey could hear the waves shushing against the shoreline.

Motionless, Hank stared out into the darkness. Lacey reached over to hold his hand, not knowing whether he would resent the intrusion or welcome the comfort.

He tightened his fingers on Lacey's. "Why is she coming here? What does she want?"

"Maybe she wants to show us all how well she's done. That's why most people go to their high school reunions." Even though she wanted to cry, Lacey used all her professional training to keep her voice calm and logical. Getting emotional wouldn't do either of them any good. They needed to think this through and prepare.

"Whatever she's here for, she's not getting her hands on my son."

"Let's not get too hasty. If it were me and I wanted to see Cody, I would have already contacted you."

"But you're not her. Jennifer never does anything up front. It's always got to be a game with her."

"I'm not taking her side, but people change. She may just want to come to the dance and razzle-dazzle us, then go back home for another ten years."

"Even so, people talk. Someone will say something and hurt my son, and I won't be able to protect him." Hank's heart raced against Lacey's ear.

"He's nine. Do you think he's never heard the rumors before?" She said it as gently as she could, but she saw Hank's face go pale in the dim light.

"I thought I could insulate him. If I was a good

enough father, no one would say anything about his lack of a mother. And then I'd never have to tell him about her. Pretty foolish, huh?"

Tenderly, Lacey recaptured Hank's hand. "What I remember about being nine is that not much escaped my notice. I'll bet Cody's given his mother plenty of thought. He may have already heard the talk around town and he's waiting for you to explain."

Hank searched the night sky. "What do I say to him?"

"You know your son better than anyone else on earth. If you were he, what would you want to hear from your father?"

"I shouldn't have to tell him anything. He's mine. Not hers, mine. Jennifer gave up any right to Cody before she even left the hospital." He scrubbed his hand through his hair. "He was so tiny, so helpless. I could cup my hands together to hold him. He hardly ever cried. He didn't have the strength. His little chest would rise and fall, then falter. He would lie so still, and I would think 'this is it.' Then he'd gulp in a mouthful of air and breathe, in and out, straining every muscle of his little body." Hank swallowed down the knot in his throat. "I've never told anyone before, but I would pretend that as long as I was sitting there next to his crib in that hospital nursery, breathing in and out, that I could breathe for him."

He stared out at the water. "I thought about adoption. For hours on end, I thought about it and prayed about it. But by the time he was out of danger, he owned a piece of my heart. I couldn't let him go." He gripped the steering wheel with both hands and buried his face on his closed fists. "What should I do?"

Lacey lay her hand on Hank's back, feeling his tension. "Why don't you call her, Hank? Ask her why she's coming."

He stiffened against her, then relaxed and whispered into the night, "You've always faced the tough stuff head on. I've always admired that about you, Lacey. Me, I'd rather wait and see if it will go away by itself. But then, trouble seems to reappear just when I've forgotten about it."

He shifted her against his shoulder and put his arms around her. "I couldn't call even if I wanted to. Jennifer's lawyer spelled out in the custody agreement that I couldn't contact her, under any circumstances. I don't know what game she's playing, but getting in touch with her would be like dealing her a hand full of aces."

"What if your lawyer called her?"

"I don't know." Hank sighed and stared up into the sky. "Look at the stars, Lacey, beaming down on us as if everything was right in the world. Are they as bright in Chicago?"

Lacey snuggled into Hank to look out the windshield at the sky above. "I can't see them from the city. The lights are too bright. I've missed them."

He rubbed his cheek against her hair. "I've missed you."

An owl hooted in the distance, while a lone cricket chirped from the truck bed. A cool wind blew through the cab, carrying the smell of moss-covered trees and rich, loamy riverbank.

Hank's breathing slowed and his heart beat steadied.

Lacey let her tears roll silently down her face, not wanting to disturb Hank by wiping them away.

And awoke to the sunrise reflecting through the mists on the river.

Chapter Seven

"Lacey? Lacey, it's morning."

The tickle in her ear woke Lacey from the deepest sleep she'd had in years. She swatted at whatever was sending those shivers down her spine and tried to recapture the end of that luscious dream.

Now where was she? Oh, yeah. Hank was whispering morning words in her ear, so tingly, so sexy, so real.

She could even smell Hank's scent, feel his touch. She stretched, luxuriating in her dream, and rammed her knee into something hard.

The remnants of her dream fled as she opened her eyes and met Hank's deep brown ones.

"Hank?"

"Good morning." He rubbed the back of his neck and ducked his head sheepishly. "We fell asleep last night."

Under other circumstances, the magnificent sunrise

out the truck's windshield would have had her in awe. Instead, she squinted in pain, as the bright sunlight reflecting off the water assaulted her scratchy eyes. Absently, she massaged her cramped shoulder while trying to make sense of her surroundings. Soft rustlings and chirping from the overhead trees played in counterpoint to the burbling of the Ouachita.

Then she remembered—and her heart sank.

Hank cranked the truck, shattering the morning's calm. "I've got to get you home. Billy is going to skin me alive."

"I'm a grown woman. My father doesn't have a right to say anything about how I spend my nights."

Hank braked and turned to her. "You gonna tell him that and break his heart?"

Lacey scrunched down in her seat. "Probably not. But then, I've probably already done that, staying out all night without even calling them."

"Billy and I have been friends for a while now. If he'll just give me a chance to explain, I'll straighten this out." Hank's words were full of bravado. It was a shame his tone of voice sounded so uncertain.

But then, it wasn't like they were lovers or anything.

His truck bounced from the dirt track to the pavement, giving Lacey an excuse to right herself and scoot over for a more solid seat.

The radio DJs, nauseatingly cheerful, chattered about the upcoming rodeo and the big sale at the Western Store. Lacey rehearsed one speech, then another in her head. Finally, she decided she'd start off with apologies for worrying her folks, then resort to tears should the situation call for them. "We both outgrew curfews a long time ago. We're adults, for heaven's sake."

Vague memories of cuddling up against Hank, practically lying on top of him, increased the pounding in her head. Scooting as far away from him as she could, she ended up against the passenger side door handle, as if that would put real distance between them.

Hank watched the road, eyes focused straight ahead. If he kept scrubbing at his neck like that, he wouldn't have an inch of skin left on it for her father to peel off.

Another worry wasn't what he needed right now.

At the house's circle drive, Hank slowed to a crawl, and coasted to a stop in front of the porch's screen door.

He leaned over the steering wheel and stared straight ahead. Lines bracketed the corners of his mouth. Then he took a deep breath. "I'll go in first and explain."

"For heaven's sake, Hank, we're not teenagers anymore. I'll go inside and apologize for not calling and everything will be fine."

"I'll walk you in." Without giving her another chance to protest, he stalked around to open the passenger door for Lacey. With stiff courtesy, he held out his hand to help her down.

"It will be all right. Don't look so guilty. We didn't do anything wrong." She sounded too desperate to even convince herself, much less Hank.

Acting on a whim, she kissed him on the cheek like she would kiss B.J. Her action might have been an innocent impulse, but her reaction was anything but innocent.

His beard rasped against her cheek and desire rasped down her spine. She rubbed her hands up and down her arms, brushing away the goose bumps, but not doing a darned thing about ridding herself of the tingle in her lips.

Hank wiped the back of his hand across his mouth, as if to wipe away her kiss. His eyes looked bleak, sad, and guilty.

She almost wished they had something to be guilty for. But they didn't.

As Hank pulled open the screen door, it screeched loud enough to wake the dead. She ducked under Hank's arm and marched into the den, where the TV blared a Sunday morning infomercial.

What was it about walking into the house that you grew up in that stripped away your maturity?

Billy had claimed the couch. His mouth hung open as he sucked in air and snored it out again. Zeb spilled over the sides of the recliner, his snore an echo of his father's, and Josh sprawled on a nest of pillows and afghans in the middle of the rug.

Although Billy and Zeb slumbered away, Josh raised himself on his elbow to study first his sister, then Hank. His unblinking, crystal cold eyes held not a single hint of sleep.

"Are you all right, Lacey?" His voice was low, quiet, lethal. Few had ever heard good-natured Josh get angry. Even fewer wanted to hear it again.

But Lacey knew how to work her little brother. She shrugged her shoulders in deliberate nonchalance and

flashed a grin. "I'm fine, no thanks to Hank. I try to se-
duce the man and he goes all noble on me and upholds
my honor or some such nonsense."

Even while Lacey watched the ice thaw in her
brother's eyes, she felt her heart sink at the near-truth in
her words.

From the depths of the couch, Billy made a disgusting
noise then stretched and opened his eyes. "Lacey?" That
single word conveyed confusion, concern and hurt.

"She's fine, Pop." Josh stood and began to fold up the
afghans. Very precisely, he straightened the edges and
laid them on a chair. "I think I'll walk Hank to the door."

Billy rubbed his swollen eyes and nodded. "Morning, Hank. I didn't see you standing there."

Hank stood at the foot of the couch, looking for all
the world like a guilty teenager caught in the act. "Nothing happened, Billy. We were just looking at the stars
and fell asleep."

Billy grinned and stood to pat Hank across the back.
"I believe you, son. I knew you'd keep my little girl safe.
Wouldn't have even waited up, except we all fell asleep
watching a John Wayne marathon. Isn't that right, Josh."

Josh grunted and pointed toward the door. Hank took
the blatant clue and took two steps toward the porch.
"I've got to get my paperwork caught up today like we
talked about, Billy. Send Cody home when he wakes
up. I'll be back to help haul the Cub to my barn this afternoon."

Lacey listened to Hank and Josh clomp down the

stairs. "Nothing happened, Pop. It was just like Hank said."

"You know, Lacey, if you keep telling me that, I might just start to think you're trying to cover up something." Billy lifted her chin so that she had to meet his gaze, eye to eye. "Baby girl, you're a grown woman and you've turned out just fine. I know you'll do what's right or have a good reason otherwise. And Hank's not the boy he used to be. I trust him."

Lacey sniffed back tears and rubbed her face into her father's chest. "I love you, Pop."

"I love you too." His arms came around her, enfolding her. She'd wished for Pop's strong, reassuring hugs a thousand times while in her lonely Chicago apartment.

Lacey heard Hank's truck crank and let out a breath she hadn't realized she was holding.

Her pop laughed as he released his bear hug. "Don't worry, baby girl. I'll bet Hank still has all his arms and legs. Josh just had to give him the brother-talk. I'm sure Hank was expecting it."

The screen door banged against the frame as Josh lumbered in, his lopsided smile back in place. "Don't make me do that again, sister."

"Who decided you were my boss?" She giggled as he rubbed the top of her head.

Lacey took stock of her six-foot-three-inch brother. No matter how big he got, he'd always be her little brother.

The recliner groaned as Zeb stretched and yawned.

"There you are, Lacey." He frowned but his sleepy attempt to look stern failed. With his hair sticking up like he'd combed it with an eggbeater and the pattern of the recliner's tweed upholstery pressed into his cheek, he looked more like a cranky toddler awakened too soon from his nap.

"Just where have you been, young lady?" He shook his finger at her, then winked at Billy. "You gonna ground her, Pop?"

She swatted at him with a throw pillow. "You'd like that wouldn't you? But you'd have to tell me how to be grounded. I don't have nearly the experience you have."

He threw the pillow back at her and scooped up another one to let fly.

Josh grabbed a few pillows from the couch and peppered his brother and sister with them. They both promptly returned the favor until Lacey spied B.J. and Cody sneaking in the doorway. "Cody! B.J! Come help me."

Although Cody held back, her youngest brother charged in, picked up a fallen pillow and lobbed it at her. "Hey! How about boys against girls?"

Lacey grabbed him and tickled his waist. "How about the big ones against the little one?"

"Cody, save me." At B.J.'s chortling plea, Cody charged in, superhero style, giggling and slinging pillows at anyone in his path. Amid squeals and belly laughs, Lacey and the twins buried B.J. and Cody in a pile of pillows. From the corner of her eye, Lacey spotted her mom standing in the doorway. Glenna watched the pillow fight, her arm around Billy's waist, her head against his shoulder. Would Lacey ever get to wear that same tender look on her face?

Then B.J. plopped the afghan over her head while Zeb chucked another pillow at B.J.

As Lacey came up for air, she heard her mom's voice break. "It's good to have them all home, isn't it? It may be a while before our whole family's under one roof again. I don't know what I'll do when they're all grown up and gone."

"I've got a few suggestions." Pop waggled his eyebrows at her and they left, observed only by Lacey. She heard their bedroom door shut, then lobbed another pillow on top of the mound covering B.J.

"Anyone want pancakes this morning?" It had been a while, but Lacey remembered where Glenna kept the pancake mix. If she tried really hard, maybe she could pretend she was cooking breakfast for Hank and Cody.

A man could only worry so much, before he had to push it all from his mind and keep on drawing breath, one lungful at the time. He hadn't been this stressed since Cody was born, but he'd survived then and he'd live through this too.

All morning, Hank focused on his paperwork and pushed all other thoughts to the back of his mind.

After lunch, with leftover spaghetti sitting heavy in his stomach, Hank crossed the Seivers' porch for the second time in one day. But this time, he didn't hesitate to knock on the door. He'd spent the morning shuffling papers and putting the Seivers back into their proper mental boxes. He was neighbor and business partner with Billy and Glenna, childhood best friends with Lacey.

Except the picture in his head of Lacey, sleep-swollen eyes, gentle smile, dawn's sunshine on her face. That memory, he couldn't quite file away for good.

It didn't help that Cody had come home bragging about how good she could cook, as if she'd invented pancakes. She'd made a big impression on his son. All morning, Cody had chattered about "Lacey this" and "Lacey that."

Because Cody left him little choice, he expanded Lacey's role in his life to include Super Sister to his son's best friend. He wished it could be more. Even if she did show some interest in him as more than a friend, he was a man with responsibilities and she was a woman with a life she loved.

B.J. answered his knock within seconds.

"Hey B.J., I need to talk with your mom." Hank held up a sheaf of papers that he had culled from his stack of paperwork. Thank heavens, it was Glenna's responsibility to fill out all the government forms.

"Okay. I'll get her. Where's Cody?"

"He's practicing staying by himself."

"Cool. My mom's gonna let me do that soon too."

The spring day wrapped around him and the porch swing called to him. He'd swung many hours on this porch. It always felt like a place he could rest and catch his breath.

Even from the porch, he heard B.J. bellow for his mom. Cody did the same thing. Why did little boys think they had to yell to be heard?

He had been so excited when Cody had said his first word. Now his son talked continuously when they were alone, even in his sleep. Like his blue eyes and blond hair, he had inherited that little personality trait from his mother. Hank just wished that Cody had inherited his mother's math sense too.

What would he do if Jennifer tried to take his son away from him? It had been so hard to leave Cody at the house by himself today, even though Hank only ran next door.

It was still hard to believe that his baby had reached the great old age of nine. Cody had wanted to stay at home by himself after school ever since he'd had his last birthday. Hank had put off the rite of passage as long as he could, but Cody had a good argument. Lots of kids stayed by themselves even younger than nine. Only none of them had been *his* son. How did a father know when to let go?

But then Hank couldn't remember wanting to break his bonds of childhood at nine. Until fourteen he'd been content to come home after school, eat a few cookies, and head off to baseball practice. All of his breaking loose had happened after his dad died.

What would he tell Cody about his mother?

"That's a grim face. Those forms must be worse than usual." Glenna came out on to the porch, a coffee cup in one hand, a can of Coke in the other. After handing the can to Hank, she pulled up an old wooden rocker and dusted off the seat.

While Hank popped the top on his drink, she sipped at her coffee and shuffled through the papers. "I'll get these filled out and in the mail. I've got your schedule worked out for the next couple of weeks. They're pretty full days. Have Cody get off the bus at our house, and he can stay here until you get home."

"I promised him that if he got an A in conduct, I'd let him stay by himself for the few hours after school until I got home." Hank swallowed half the can in one gulp. "I think it's the first A he's ever made. Not even a check mark for talking too much."

"Sounds like you're stuck, then. He'll be fine, Hank. And so will you." Glenna brushed a gray strand of hair from her face. "I've survived through raising three and have one to go. Cody's a lot more sensible than Josh and Zeb put together at that age."

"It's just so hard to let go. And now, with Jennifer coming to town . . ." Hank leaned back in the swing, making the chains rattle. When would he stop questioning his decision to raise Cody alone? Glenna and Billy told him, almost daily, that he was doing a fine job of it. When would he start believing them?

"We don't have any reason to be alarmed yet." Glenna patted him on the knee. "If you don't let your children go, they'll break away from you. Then you might not get them back." She shoved up from her rocking chair. "Come on in while I grab those other papers you need to sign."

Glenna stopped short of the screen door and Hank had to do a fancy two-step to keep from plowing into her. She turned to face him, "One more thing, Hank— about *my* child. I don't want to see Lacey hurt."

Heaviness blanketed Hank's heart at the thought of causing Lacey pain. "I'd rather cut off my right arm than hurt Lacey."

"Just remember who you'll answer to." She pinned him with a deadly serious stare. "And I'm not talking about her brothers."

He couldn't answer past the lump in his throat. He hoped his solemn expression would tell Glenna that he understood. She grabbed his hand and gave it a little squeeze, then headed off toward her sewing room-turned-office.

He trailed behind, until the soft sobs coming from the den stopped him short.

Peeking in the doorway, he saw Lacey, curled up on the couch sobbing into the tail of her oversized T-shirt.

Oh, no. This had to be *his* fault for last night's care-lessness. He wavered between doing the safe thing and following Glenna into her office or checking on Lacey.

Next thing he knew, he was down on his knees next to the couch, drying Lacey's tears with his hand. "Lacey, I'm sorry. I was supposed to take care of you. I didn't mean to fall asleep."

"Sh!" She pointed to the TV screen. While "Un-chained Melody" played in the background, ghostly Patrick Swayze leaned over Demi Moore, giving her a phantom kiss that she would never feel. "I can't think of anything worse than loving someone and that person not even knowing you existed."

"I don't think you'd ever have to worry about that, Lacey. Any man who would overlook you would be as dumb as a stump." Hank would give a year of his life to know how to interpret the look Lacey shot him. At least it stopped her tears.

She sat up on the couch and flicked the pause button on the remote control. "I've decided that all men have wood for brains. Don't you agree?"

The smile she sent him, mouth curved like an angel's but eyes flashing with a devilish glint, gave him the correct answer.

"Yes." He swallowed and forced his own unsure smile. "I think you might have figured us out. If only women were so easy to understand."

B.J. burst into the room, hurdled a mound of floor pillows, and came to a halt next to the couch. "Is the mushy part over?"

Hank jerked up his head, not realizing until that instant that his mouth had been scant millimeters from Lacey's.

Lacey smoothed down the hem of her T-shirt. "You know, B.J., some things are over before they even begin."

Hank felt as puzzled as B.J. looked. He wanted to imagine that Lacey had just made a play for him, but he knew in his heart that it was just his imagination.

Then she blinked and dislodged a tear from her lashes.

B.J. scooted between Hank and Lacey, stepping on

Hank's toes. "Lace, Pop says to ask you if you remember how to drive the tractor? He wants to know if you can pull Hank's Cub back to his barn."

Lacey broke into a real smile, one with no hidden meanings. "You tell Pop that the day I forget how to drive a tractor is the day I'll have to start calling myself a city girl. Go sign your papers, Hank, and I'll meet you in the shop."

Lacey bounced along the grass trek between her pop's shop and Hank's barn, wincing as her butt slapped the hard tractor seat. She drove so slowly she had to site off the trees to make sure she was moving. Behind her, Hank's Cub skipped and hopped on the end of the chain with Hank in the cockpit. She didn't dare turn around and stare at him, but she knew he was back there watching her, or maybe she only hoped he watched her.

Awareness of Hank screamed up and down her nerves. Unrequited love sounded so romantic when the poets sang its praises. It hurt like no tomorrow when you had to live it.

She had thought she could get him out of her head by seeing him again. Instead he had become firmly embedded in her heart. And he was stomping around in there with his cleats on.

After too much time to think, she finally pulled up to Hank's barn that doubled as his hanger. With the doors already opened on both ends, she drove in and through, stopping so the Cub came to rest securely in the middle.

The back door of the house slammed closed as Cody

hurtled out and ran for the barn. He bounced near the cockpit door, excitement in every jump. "Dad! Dad!"

Hank climbed from the cockpit and caught his son in mid-leap. "Well? Did you keep the homefront safe?"

"Yeah, but I heard a noise!" Cody's eyes behind his glasses grew so big they took up most of his face. "I called Mrs. Glenna and she said you'd be right here. Then I checked the icemaker and found out the noise was just a tray of ice dumping. That was smart thinking to look in the freezer, wasn't it, Dad?"

"Yup, you did fine, son."

"You *were* smart to think of the icemaker, even though you were, uh, worried." Thank goodness, Lacey had stopped herself from saying the word, *scared* to a nine-year-old. She had a hard enough time getting Cody to talk around her without insulting him when he finally did.

"How much math homework did you get done?" Hank wiped his son's smile clean off the boy's face.

"I just can't do it. It's too hard." If Cody stuck his lip out any further, it would drag the ground.

Lacey wanted to hug the boy and make it all better, but at nine, Cody wouldn't appreciate her outburst of affection. He might not appreciate her offer to help either, but she would give it a try anyway. "I'm fairly good with math. Can I look at it?"

Cody glanced at Lacey, then Hank, then back to Lacey. "Sure. But I gotta warn you, they're fractions—and they're all word problems."

Maybe the pillow fight and the pancakes had helped

win Cody over or maybe the math problems were worth letting down his guard. Whatever the answer, Lacey felt a load lift from her shoulders when Cody accepted her offer.

"I've worked a few fraction word problems in my time. Let's see what you got."

"Okay! Follow me!" Cody sprinted from the barn, looking back over his shoulder to make sure Lacey trailed behind him. When he saw that Lacey still stood next to his dad, he slowed his normal trot to a standstill and called out, "Are you coming?"

"Looks like I've got homework to do."

"Better you than me." Hank grinned, flashing his dimple at her. "I've got a few things to do out here. I'll catch up with you in a few minutes."

Cody waited for Lacey, obviously worried that if he let her out of his sight, he would lose his tutor. He even held the door for her, a sure sign that he was desperate.

An open math book, assorted pens and pencils, and a ream of paper, most of the pages covered in sketches of comic book heroes, littered the kitchen table.

"Let's get this knocked out, okay?" Lacey picked up a wadded paper ball from the kitchen chair next to Cody's and sat. This lesson wasn't just about math. She wanted Cody to like her. The boy was her little brother's best friend and Hank's son. And, more importantly, he was a good kid, a child who was fast claiming a place in her heart right next to his father's.

A pitcher of tea later, Lacey and Cody had completed his homework, five whole word problems. Hank had retreated to his office ten minutes after they started. No question that Cody had inherited his math phobia from his dad.

"This is a stupid assignment. When will I ever use fractions?" Cody pushed his glasses up and sneered at the paper. Lines and lines of fractions marched in crooked rows across his paper.

"All the time. I'll prove it to you."

"How can you prove it?"

"We'll make brownies, but we'll change the recipe by using fractions. Now, do you want more brownies or less brownies?"

"More, of course. Dad likes brownies, and so do I."

"Then let's make three-fourths more than we usually do." Lacey searched the pantry for ingredients and placed a hasty call home when she couldn't find cocoa. While they waited on their emergency delivery, she and Cody figured, measured, and mixed the rest of the ingredients.

B.J. crashed into the Chandler kitchen, puffing from running the whole distance and triumphantly bearing the cocoa can like the Olympic torch.

"You pay the delivery guy in brownies, right?" He held the can out of Lacey's reach until she agreed to his price.

Laughing, she agreed to his price as she made a swipe for the can. "You learned that trick from Josh, didn't you?"

The boys made paper airplanes from Cody's superhero sketches, and Lacey mixed in the cocoa and daydreamed about having a family.

Heavy footsteps warned her of Hank's approach, but not in time to disperse the last of her silly musings.

"If I promise to clean up, can I have a brownie too?" Hank's deep voice fit perfectly in her little fantasy. Then he aimed his dimpled smile at Lacey, and she dropped the spoon in the thick goo.

Nothing dispelled a good fantasy better than a dirty kitchen. Deliberately, she studied the mess she and Cody had made. "Cleaning up in here is worth at least one brownie. In fact, I'll even let you lick the bowl when I'm through."

For a fleeting second, she thought Hank would drop a kiss on her nose. Instead he grabbed the mixing spoon, stuck out his tongue, and cleaned off a dollop of brownie mix. How could Hank have looked so sexy just by licking a mixing spoon free of chocolate?

Lacey hid her fascination by running a sink of hot water. She squirted in the soap, wishing she could wash away her misplaced desire for her best friend as easily as she washed away the butter and sugar residue. A relationship with Hank just wasn't practical. He had come so far to build a business that he loved in a town that respected him. She couldn't see uprooting Cody and taking him away from everyone who loved him.

And she had her own career. How could she throw away all the studying, all the hours, and all the connections she had worked so hard to cultivate and that were so essential to a lawyer's success? She had everything she had always wanted—except Hank. Deep down inside, she accepted that she would never be able to scrub away her craving to see desire flame in Hank's chocolate-brown eyes.

Lacey plunged her hands into the hot, soapy water and gave the chocolate-coated pot a scrubbing it wouldn't forget. No matter how hard she concentrated on washing the pot, she couldn't stop the quick glances she kept sneaking at Hank. She felt so foolish, so silly for not having more control. But she was aware of his every move, his every breath even halfway across the room, elbow-deep in dirty dishwater.

The phone rang and Hank gave his spoon one last dart of his tongue before answering. He turned his back to Lacey when he reached for the receiver so he missed seeing the delicious, frightening shudder that raced down Lacey's spine and made her hands tremble so badly that she sloshed soap bubbles over the sides of the sink onto the counter.

Before she could recapture her composure, Hank hung up the receiver. "That was Billy. He wants you to bring home his tire gauge." He dug the little tool from a kitchen drawer and set it on the table. Until the day she died, she bet that tire gauges would represent painful conversations.

"Where'd that smile go?" Swiping a bite of brownie from Lacey's plate, he held it up to her mouth. "I know. You need more chocolate. Take a bite?"

"Sure." This was as close as she would ever come to her dream of eating wedding cake from his fingers.

His fingers touched her lips, and this time, she couldn't stop her shivers. Her knees began to buckle as every bone in her body turned into liquid warmth. She had to lean hard against the counter before she hit the floor.

"Good?"

"Wonderful."

"I think so too." He leaned toward her, so close that Lacey was certain he was about to kiss her. But then he blinked and backed away. "Now let me at those dishes. I've got a kitchen to clean."

She couldn't do it. She couldn't think of Hank as just a friend. Finger-feeding and near-miss kisses aside, what woman could help but love a man with dishpan hands?

Chapter Eight

Hank closed the cabinet door on the last mixing bowl and listened to Lacey and the boys giggle as they hunted for paper airplanes from behind the den chairs and couch. A crumpled plane sailed into the kitchen to land under the table.

With her eyes sparkling and her face flushed, she appeared in the doorway. "Pardon me, sir, but did you see a slightly off-course jet land in here?"

"I think I saw one touch down right under there." As he pointed, he saw her gaze follow his direction, then focus on the tire gauge. He snatched it up and stuck it in his pocket before the offending tool could bring that sad look to her face again. How long would it be before she forgot how he'd humiliated her before the whole ballpark? Would it help if he sent her flowers?

"I guess I need to get that gauge back to Pop soon."

She held out her hand and, for the first time ever, he noticed how delicate her fingers were.

"I'll walk over with you. I need to put some time into the new plane we're building, anyway. So far, with the weather so good for spraying, Billy's had to do most of the construction by himself and we're a few weeks behind schedule."

The walk between the two houses normally took ten minutes, at a snail's pace. He tried to stretch it any way he could. He might not have forever with Lacey, but he had today.

He encouraged the boys to stop and throw rocks into the ditches; he pointed out all the wildflowers to Lacey; he inspected bugs that landed on those wildflowers and anything else he could think of to make this walk last longer.

As they strolled along, he made sure his fingers brushed her hair from her face, or covered her hand as he pointed to a bird, or touched her back as they leaned over to inspect a crawfish mound. Could Lacey feel the prickle like he did? If she *did* feel it, did she think it was a good thing or a bad thing? Right now, he didn't want to know. He just wanted this contentment to last forever and either answer, yes or no, would complicate their lives.

The day was perfect, just enough breeze to stay cool and keep the mosquitoes at bay, just enough sun to keep the chill bumps away. Birds sang, bees buzzed, and frogs croaked. The air smelled of fresh cut grass and flowers in bloom. Days like these made Hank feel good about his decision to raise Cody here, right where he grew up, instead of following his brother's family to Gulf Shores.

Everyone but Billy and Glenna had said he was a rash teenager for attempting to raise Cody himself, but he and Cody would have been two more mouths to feed as Rob struggled to care for their sickly mother while trying to establish a family with his newlywed bride. He'd picked up enough jobs around the airport to feed his son, with Billy filling in the gaps with odd jobs here and there.

After ten long years, Rob and his wife had three children and good careers. Mom loved her new friends in the retirement home and the daily stroke rehabilitation sessions continued to work miracles. Hank was master of his own destiny, and Cody was healthy and happy.

But then, Jennifer would be here soon.

Thick, puffy clouds floated in front of the sun, turning his world gray and making him shiver. Spring storms were building beyond the horizon.

With a start, Hank realized he didn't even remember walking those last fifty yards.

"Thanks for the escort home." Lacey dug her shoe in the shingle tabs, drawing a big H, then erasing it with one sideways sweep of her foot. Without doubt, that H was for *home,* not for *Hank.*

He had the strongest urge to kiss her good-bye, like they'd been on a date or something. Instead, he swiped his hand across his mouth. "Sure, any time."

Without a backward glance, Lacey headed for the house, leaving Hank wishing for a simpler life—a life where he could kiss her any time he liked, and where he'd never have to say good-bye.

But they were just friends. Why did he have such a hard time remembering that?

From the open double doors, Hank watched his son shove his best friend from the tractor seat.

Billy joined him in the doorway, chewing on his sucker stick. He pointed with his stick toward the tractor. "Reminds me of you and Lacey at that age."

Hank nodded agreement. Although burying his grown-up desires for her just might do him in, he'd keep their friendship simple and uncomplicated if it killed him.

"Did I tell you Cody's got to take math over in summer school? I don't think I'll ever get this parenting thing right."

"Seems to me, I recall Cody's father doing the same thing in fourth grade." Billy patted Hank on the shoulder. "You've been doing fine, so far. Your first kid is always an experiment anyway. Get three or four underfoot and you don't have time to worry about doing it right. You're too busy worrying about just doing it." Billy gave Hank a sideways glance. "Of course, you've got to find a woman to do it with first."

Hank flinched. He had heard the bite of this lecture many times before. It wasn't that he didn't want to find a woman to share his life with. He had just made such a terrible mistake the first time around. And he'd never even gotten to the marriage part, just the proposing part. Of course, calling Jennifer by Lacey's name hadn't helped matters.

Billy leaned against the open doorframe and stared out at the pasture. "I seem to remember from years past that taking a pretty lady to dinner can be quite enjoyable."

The tractor coughed then rumbled to life.

The familiar tug between parental duty and loneliness yanked Hank's conscience. "It's hard to leave Cody with a sitter at night when I spend so much time away from him, especially this time of year."

"We enjoy having Cody spend the night. Glenna and I feel like he's part ours. With the twins moving out, it'll be too quiet around here." Billy shaded his eyes from the bright sun. "Jennifer was a long time ago, Hank. You're older now and, hopefully, wiser. Keeping to himself isn't good for a man."

Hank didn't know about good for him, but it was certainly safer.

Lacey spent the evening curled up in bed enjoying a good book. For the first time since last Christmas, she didn't feel the slightest twinge of guilt for taking time to read for pleasure instead of studying briefs.

She'd bought this book because the medieval knight on the cover had a dimple like Hank's and the princess's hair was honey-gold like hers.

She read into the wee hours, enjoying the luxury of vacation.

When the Anglo-Saxon princess vowed to always love

her Norman knight in shining armor, Lacey cheered and turned out her light.

When she awoke the early morning sun was shining through her curtains and making shifting patterns on her bedroom walls.

She stretched, feeling as sensuous as a cat, despite her oversized sleepshirt and mascara-stuck eyelids.

The buzz of an airplane motor drifted through Lacey's open bedroom window. She rose up on one elbow and squinted at the numbers on her clock. Six forty-two? In the morning?

She pushed back the curtain and saw the first pink shafts of sunlight across the field. In the dawn light, Hank's yellow Cub looked like a black smudge silhouetted against the fluffy white clouds that skipped across the pastel sky.

Chatter floated into her room, reminding her that Hank wasn't the only one with an early schedule. Her mom would have been up for a few hours, scheduling deliveries of fertilizers at the fields, ordering parts for Pop, cooking breakfast, and getting B.J. ready for school. Glenna did more work before 8:00 than most folks did all day.

Brakes groaned and squealed and the front door slammed amid B.J.'s cries of "Bye, Mom. Later, Pop."

Without even looking, Lacey knew the big yellow school bus sat at the end of the drive, most likely the same bus that had carried her and Hank to school.

Lacey rolled from the bed and shuffled to the bathroom, only to run up against a locked door. She pounded until the shower quit, then yelled through the door. "Leave me some hot water."

"Too late." Zeb's cheerful voice called back. Knowing the wait could be half a minute to half an hour, she padded to her parents' room to use their little half-bath.

Although the curtains and bedspread had changed over the years, the feeling of warmth stayed the same. Picture frames and loose change covered the dresser top, and a crayon drawing from Cody's kindergarten years fluttered from the mirror. Framed drawings from Zeb's, Josh's and her early years decorated the walls next to professional paintings of the French countryside.

The amateur artwork looked distinctly different than the paintings Mom had picked up from the sidewalks of Paris. That's where Pop had met Mom when she had been studying to be an art appraiser. Pop joked that he had to go all the way to France to find an American girl who would marry him. She'd taken one glance at the dashing Air Force airplane mechanic and had left her dream world of glitz and art.

Glenna often told them that she wouldn't trade a second of the time she'd had with Pop or her children to spend a decade at some old musty museum, and Lacey believed her.

Lacey zipped up her blue denim shorts and pulled on her faded peach tank top. A quick and easy ponytail completed her grooming. When she swung her head, the ends tickled her bare back. After her daily routine of stockings and business suits, she felt like she'd escaped from a straitjacket.

Glenna insisted on cooking every morning except Sundays, so Lacey readied her stomach for eggs and biscuits. From the smell of things, bacon had made the menu too. The big spread was a far cry from her city breakfast of Diet Coke and a vending machine bagel. Her stomach growled in anticipation, and she vowed to ignore the bathroom scales until she got back to Chicago.

The kitchen was empty but the table was full, as Lacey's nose had warned her. With her plate loaded, she headed out to the porch where Mom and Pop sat on the swing, side by side, and sipped from their coffee cups. The wooden planks felt cool on her bare feet as she headed for an empty rocker.

Billy looked over the top of his newspaper at her.

"Well, look who's finally awake."

Finally? A quick glance through the screen door at the VCR clock proved that it was only 7:45.

"Now Billy, Lacey's entitled to sleep in on vacation, although I am glad you're up. As soon as you're done with breakfast, I need you to try on your evening gown so I can check the fit and pin the hem."

The bite Lacey chewed turned from crisp bacon to shoe leather in her mouth. The reunion dance. She could imagine what the most talked about topic would be—Jennifer and Hank. After the ballpark kiss, the gossips might even throw her name into the rumor mill too. It didn't help that she would be attending alone.

Lacey lifted her chin. The grown-up Lacey Seivers went where she wanted to go, when she wanted to go there, no matter who snickered behind her back. She would attend that dance, come hell or high water.

Besides, after all the work her mother had done making her dress, how could Lacey back out on attending? "Sure thing, Mom. I can't wait to see it."

But she couldn't make herself swallow another bite of breakfast.

After stashing her plate in the sink, Lacey met Glenna in the corner of her combination sewing room and business office.

Glenna held up a scrap of shiny material to catch the light. Lacey watched the color shimmer a brilliant sapphire blue as it slithered in her mother's hand. The thin fabric moved like liquid silk.

"I've got it finished except for the hem," Glenna said. "Slip on the shoes you plan to wear with it and try it on. I need to see how it fits."

Lacey unfolded from her cross-legged position on the floor and examined the bit of cloth fluttering from her mother's fingers. "That's a scarf, right? Or maybe a belt tie?"

Her mom arched an eyebrow. "No, young lady. It's the evening gown you sent me the pattern to make."

Glenna handed the pattern envelope to Lacey. Right next to the formfitting halter dress her mom had made was the conservative, high-necked, full-skirted gown Lacey thought she would be wearing. "But I meant this one."

"Oh, honey, I thought you told me the one on the left. I don't have time to make another one. Why don't you try it on? I think it will show off your best assets."

"Well, Mom, I think this dress will show not only my assets but everything else I usually keep covered."

Carefully, apprehensively, she wiggled into the dress. The slinky material covered all her strategic places—barely.

"Glenna. Phone!" Pop bellowed from the den, probably deafening the person on the other end of the line.

"I'll be right back, honey. Don't move. I need to pin the hem."

Lacey turned to face the full length mirror and a stranger stared back from the beveled glass.

Not only had Lacey never had a dress like this, she'd never even tried one on for grins and giggles.

It draped low in the back, dipping to the bottom of her spine. The sapphire material fit like a second skin, turning her hips and thighs into graceful curves. If she had to pick only one word to describe the dress, and herself in it, that word would be *elegant.*

What would Hank do if he were to see her in this dress? What did she want him to do?

"I did do a good job on this one, didn't I?" Glenna looked well satisfied with herself. "It fits you perfectly."

"Yes, it does." Lacey turned to check out her backside view again in the mirror. "Great job, Mom. A thousand thanks."

"You're welcome. I felt like a real couturier." Glenna

eyed the ballet flats on Lacey's feet. "I need to hem it with the shoes you're going to wear with it."

"I forgot to pack the shoes. I'll need to run into town and pick up a pair."

"Uh-oh. I really need to start working on the hem. Stand still a second." Glenna headed toward her room and came back carrying a pair of strappy sandals. "I found these in my closet. They're basic black, nothing special, but the heel height looks about right."

Lacey slipped on the shoes, thankful that she and her mom had shared a shoe size since her teens.

Glenda knelt down to pin the hem. Then she cleared her throat, a sure sign of a serious discussion on the agenda. "I've been meaning to talk to you about Saturday night. Or maybe I should say Sunday morning."

With Lacey's dress hem firmly clutched in her hands, Glenna sure knew how to pick her moments.

"Nothing happened, Mom."

"That's what I wanted to talk to you about." Glenna twirled her daughter so Lacey faced away from the mirror. "You're a grown woman and you can stay out all night if you want to."

"But I should have called. I know you were worried."

"Not very. You were safe with Hank—which is what I really wanted to talk to you about. Hank's turned into a fine man." Glenna adjusted a pin. "He's practically part of the family now. I know he's had your heart since you were a teenager. The way you look at him, anyone can see you still feel that way about him. And every time he looks at you, his eyes take on a certain spark."

"Do they really?"

"Yes, they do. It would be so easy for him to fall in love with you. I think he's just waiting for some encouragement from you. But honey, his life's work is here. And your's is in Chicago. One of you would have to give up an awful lot. I don't want to see either of you hurt. But I *do* want to see both of you happy."

"What should I do?" Lacey searched her mother's face for the answers.

"I wish I could tell you what to do, but I can't. Even if I had an answer, it's your life, baby girl. I want to tell you to be careful, but sometimes careful isn't the right answer, either." Glenna pushed a strand of hair behind her daughter's ear. "Know that my ears and arms are always open for you."

"Glenna? Have you seen the tractor keys?" Pop burst through the doorway. He did a double take at Lacey. "Won't you be cold in that dress?"

Glenna fished Pop's keys from her jeans pocket and handed them to him, along with a frowned warning that Lacey wasn't supposed to see. "She'll be dancing with so many men, she'll stay plenty warm."

A chill ran down Lacey's spine. She was pretty sure that only one man could warm her heart, and she didn't even know if she wanted him to set the fire.

Chapter Nine

"What do you think?" Glenna looked up at her daughter as she stuck the last pin in place, her forehead wrinkled in concern.

"It's fabulous, absolutely stunning." How could Lacey say anything else when each and every stitch was perfect?

"Good! I'll turn up the hem this afternoon and it will be done." Glenna stood up, put her hands on her hips, and arched her back. "Could you run an errand for me?"

"Sure, Mom."

"Hank's spraying some Louisiana Extension Service fields and they want to change the flow rate on this afternoon's fields. Hank doesn't have the nozzles for the new rate. After I fix up the paperwork, could you run them out to him? Your father can draw a map to get you there."

"Sure, I'll be glad to." Lacey's thoughts whirled. What a morning to go barefaced! Did she have time for makeup? And what about her hair? Lacey shook off her silly worries. She was on vacation, after all. And Hank had seen her looking a lot worse than she looked right now. She wasn't trying to impress him. No, she took that back. Of course she wanted to impress Hank. She just didn't know where she wanted it to lead.

Her plan had been so simple. Fulfill family obligations, enjoy some downtime, and put Hank in his place as a childhood friend from days gone by. Instead Hank was trying to take a new place in her heart—and she wasn't sure if it was on purpose or not. This situation was getting more complicated than a three-hundred-page legal brief.

She had vowed not to think of the office while she was in West Monroe, but she was about to break that vow. She might not be able to untangle her feelings about Hank, but she could certainly bury them in a pile of work. It's a technique she had practiced since high school. She should check her office email as soon as she finished her errand.

While she waited on Billy's directions, she ran a brush through her hair, then decided a ponytail might work best to present a casual, "just friends" demeanor. Of course, lipstick was a necessity since her mouth had suddenly gone dry. The touch of blush and double coat of mascara was only to fill her time while she waited on Pop. Fifteen minutes later, she studied her father's napkin artwork. "Explain this map to me, Pop, and I'll be on my way. What's this squiggly thing next to the big tree?"

With her lashes darkened and thickened, the lightest touch of blush on her cheeks, and peach lipstick on her lips, Lacey climbed into her Pop's old red Chevy, now faded to pink, and began her forty-five-minute trek to the fields near the Columbia River. The old truck bounced over the asphalt roads, jostling her until her teeth rattled. She'd learned to drive in this truck, bucking up and down the driveway and grinding the gears as she figured out when to push in the clutch.

The radio speakers blared out country classics and she blared right back, singing so loud her Chicago neighbors would have been banging on the apartment walls. She even rolled down the window and let the rushing air tie her ponytail into knots. The smell of piney-woods and newly turned fields more than made up for her tangled hair. She'd run a brush through it before Hank saw her.

She gave a fleeting thought to what everyone must be doing at work. Had the senior partners approved her presentation? Or was Todd stealing her case, even now? Even though she tried to muster up indignation, or even worry, the beautiful day kept her too distracted.

Each mile held a different wonder. She watched a hawk fly overhead, swooping low over the fields to find its prey. A Black Angus cow stuck her head through the strands of fencing, trying to reach a clump of scarlet clover that grew in the ditch barely out of her reach.

Two young colts raced around their water barrel, kicking up their heels and celebrating life.

Almost regretfully, Lacey slowed down to search for her turnoff. Thankfully Pop drew a darned good map or she would have missed the dirt trail that abruptly veered off the main road. Navigating the big truck down the narrow ruts that masqueraded as a path caused her to miss a word or two of the current song, but she regained her beat soon enough and bleated out the words, making up the ones she didn't know.

As she neared the levy, she spotted a plane that seemed to spring from the earth. The yellow Cub climbed straight up, swooped into a 180-degree turn, then dived back, nose first, toward the field. Just as Lacey thought Hank would crash into the black loam, he leveled out and let loose his spray. From where she sat, the belly of the plane seemed to brush the ground. Misty fog sprayed from the back of the plane in a V, floating in the air before settling on the crops.

A tree row marked the end of the field. Lacey held her breath as Hank seemed to brush the limbs of the trees in his ascent. He looped over, like he was flying along the edge of a bow ribbon. Watching him perform the tricky maneuver made her heart pound into her throat. Again he plunged toward the tilled soil, down, down.

Lacey stuffed her fist into her mouth and closed her eyes, sure he would crash, but the motor buzz never faltered. When she built up enough courage to look again, Hank was flying level, scant yards from the ground.

Hank's exhibition thrilled, fascinated, and frightened Lacey. And he flew like this every day, all day, not just every now and then like those adrenaline junkies who got their thrills from extreme sports. Until this very second, she hadn't realized that the profession Hank talked of incessantly, that he loved, was so dangerous.

Lacey unclenched her hands from the steering wheel and drove toward the group of trucks parked down the road. The Chevy crept forward, barely above idle speed. She needed all the time she could squeeze to regain her composure.

Hank had to fly low, the lower the better. Logically, she knew that controlling overspray not only saved the farmer money by cutting down on the amount of chemical he needed, it also saved the environment from unnecessary exposure.

Well, Hank certainly was making some conservative farmers happy.

Not able to look away, Lacey watched him skim the field, barely missing an irrigation stand.

Did he have to be so darned conscientious?

Some days were made for flying. Hank pulled back on the throttle and cleared the tree row. The Cub responded like an extension of his hand. He couldn't have felt freer if he'd had wings.

Flying did more than put shoes on his son's feet, it put joy in his soul. How many men got to experience a rush like this every day at work? A small handful at most. There was no doubt he was one of fortune's sons.

From his lofty perch, he watched Billy's pick-up bounce down the tractor row. Billy must have sent Zeb or Josh with the nozzles.

The warm sunshine made him yawn and he compensated to keep the plane steady. He'd been awake most of the night, trying to figure out what to do next. Between Lacey and Jennifer, he hadn't even closed his eyes. At least he'd figured out what to do about Jennifer. He would talk to Cody, tell him anything he wanted to know, answer all his questions, and tell him, over and over again, how much he loved his son. He'd had that one figured out before midnight.

The rest of the night, he'd tried to decide what to do about his attraction to Lacey. All he'd ended up doing was wadding his sheets into a knot. Just like his emotions.

On the instrument panel, his idiot light flickered to remind him that his hopper was empty. He shouldn't have needed the reminder. He should have known his load was spent long before that light came on. Good thing it hadn't been his stall indicator instead. At this altitude he would have had no choice but to ride her in.

When would he learn that thinking of Lacey while he flew could be dangerous? He *must* keep his mind on his job.

Hank yanked up on the stick and climbed, banked for his turn, a sloppy shondelle, and glided back down over the field.

As he scanned the fields below, he watched the truck pull to a stop near the agents. When Lacey emerged from the cab, he blinked twice to be sure he wasn't still daydreaming. From his vantage point, she seemed to be all legs and glorious hair. Her silky ponytail swung in counterpoint to her hips as she walked to the group of farm agents.

Hank touched down on the part of the field left unplanted just for him. He taxied to a stop near the portable chemical holding tank and climbed out, taking his time and trying to get his thoughts back to business.

The group of agents started toward him, with Lacey in the lead. She had such a beautiful walk, big, effortless steps that covered ground and had her hips swaying in that strut that only long-legged women could manage.

How many men in Chicago noticed her walk? Did they come out of their tiny offices to watch her glide down the hall? Of course they must. How could they help themselves?

"I'm impressed!" Lacey's shout reached him over the dying motor. "That was quite a show."

"Why, thank you, ma'am. I worried that you'd want your money back." He tipped his baseball cap, pretending like they were still just friends like twenty years ago, like two days ago.

Then she licked her lips and all thoughts of childhood left him. His hands began to sweat and his head started to throb.

One of the agents winked at Lacey before turning to Hank. "We're sure glad this little lady could bring out your equipment, Hank. It's rare that I get to visit with a pretty girl while on the job. And it looks like she brought us exactly what we need, even new paperwork to cover the new flow rate. One of the things we like best about your outfit is the way you handle all the forms and such." The man patted Lacey on the shoulder, then folded the paperwork and stuck it in his shirt pocket.

Hank kept his answer strictly business. "All the credit goes to my general manager, Glenna Seivers."

The agent took off his cowboy hat and swiped his hand across his brow, ignoring Hank and focusing on Lacey. "Sure is hot for this time of year. Hope that rain comes in tomorrow like it's predicted, though I imagine it might mess up your vacation plans. My daughter plans to lie around our pool every blessed day of her spring break, even with the weather blowing in like this. Says she needs herself a tan to catch a good husband."

All the men around him chuckled like he's just told a funny joke, a sure sign that he was the boss. That was another thing Hank liked about his job, he was his own boss.

The agent smiled at being given his due. "I imagine you're about her age. Which college do you go to, little lady?"

Hank risked a glance at Lacey to see how she handled being called a little lady.

She chewed on her lip and twirled her ponytail around her finger like a young debutante, then blinked up at the agent through her lashes. "I've been out of college a few years now. I didn't get to do a lot of sitting by the pool at Notre Dame."

The man raised his eyebrows and resettled his hat.

"Notre Dame, huh? They've got a pretty good football team. What'd you major in, honey?"

"I majored in history."

"And what does a history major do when she graduates?"

"She goes to law school then gets a job with a great big law firm." Lacey flashed him a cutesy smile.

The man gave her a wink and chuckled, nudging his companions to get them to join in, as if Lacey told the joke this time.

Was Hank the only one who realized the agent had just been put in his place for patronizing her?

The old Lacey from high school would have ducked her head, overcome with shyness, and mumbled a two-word reply. But this Lacey, the one with big city polish, had learned a thing or two about handling people.

Hank wished she would handle him, hold him, hug him, never let him go. But it was hard to hold hands from West Monroe to Chicago, much less build a relationship.

The agent mopped his forehead again, then turned his attention back to Hank and to business. "With these showers we're expecting, are you gonna have both this field and the one down the road done before dark?"

"So far, I'm on schedule. I plan to stay out here until they get done."

"Just see you don't fly over your limit. I don't want the FAA coming down on the Louisiana Extension Service."

"I'd rather not have them coming down on me, either. I always do things by the book."

"That's why we hire you, boy." He looked around to

his audience. "Y'all want to go to the diner for a cup of coffee? I'll buy. You, too, little lady."

"No thanks, I've got to get home to lay out by the pool before it rains tomorrow."

"See. What'd I tell you, men? All these young women like to soak up the sunshine. Got to look good to make those boyfriends pop the question." He kept up a string of nonsense as he and his cronies headed back across the field to their trucks.

The thought of Lacey married to someone else made Hank nauseous. The thought of Lacey, alone and lonely, broke his heart.

When they were out of earshot, Lacey broke into a grin. "What do you think, Hank? With a good tan, do you think I could catch a husband?"

"If you let the word get out that you were looking for one, men would be lined up from West Monroe to Calhoun, waiting their turn to propose."

Giving him the same outrageous, over-the-top look she'd cast at the agent, she dramatically fluttered her lashes and said, "Would you be in that line, Hank?"

Even though Lacey's question was meant in fun, Hank's nerve endings balled up between his shoulder blades. He'd like to know the answer to that question himself.

Jennifer Myers parked her vintage 450L Mercedes deep in the shadows of a live oak tree across the street from Judson Tyler Elementary School's deserted playground, pulled out her binoculars, and settled in to wait for the fourth-grade class's recess. The approaching cold front sent an occasional breeze through the open windows, but she wouldn't interrupt her surveillance long enough to reach for her blue denim jacket in the back seat.

Twenty minutes later, a buzzer sounded and dozens of children ran onto the playing field. She compared the quickly moving faces with the grainy black and white picture that her private investigator had taken a few days ago until she spotted a match.

Her heart sped and her hands shook so badly that she couldn't keep the binoculars focused. She wiped at her eyes, took a deep calming breath, then refocused the lenses.

She followed the boy's every movement until the buzzer sounded again and they all trooped back in. Then with clumsy fingers, she punched in a long distance number on her cell phone.

Finally, on the ninth ring, he answered.

"Jennifer? You made the trip okay?" Steve's deep, steady voice calmed her.

She cleared the excitement from her throat and bypassed the hellos. "I saw him, just like I told you I would. They haven't changed the recess schedule since I was in school. This town never changes."

The phone crackled in the silence, then, "Don't do anything foolish."

"I love you, Steve." Jennifer broke the connection, cranked her car, and pulled it into the school's parking lot. She checked her makeup in the rearview mirror, reached for the door handle, then pulled her hand back as if the metal burnt her hand.

Cautiously, slowly, she restarted her car and headed toward her old street and the house she'd left ten years ago.

Chapter Ten

Lacey lay back among the bubbles, trying to soak away the tension gripping her neck. She wasn't having much success thinking of Hank as just a friend and now, to add to the problem, Donna Sue had offered her an option that she couldn't seem to shrug off.

Over the past several years, Donna Sue had built up a nice, small town legal practice. Now West Monroe was growing and so was Donna Sue's family.

On the way back home, Donna Sue had spotted Lacey at the red light and called her over to have coffee. They had spent a delightful fifteen minutes comparing big corporate offices to small, single-owner offices. Somewhere near the bottom of the cup, Donna Sue ever so casually mentioned that she would be cutting back her practice.

She'd asked if Lacey knew anyone who might want to trade in big money, big city, and big pressures for a small-town partnership. While she'd been careful to make the question broad enough to give Lacey a graceful way to ignore the offer, she'd made it pretty clear that she intended to partner with someone, and the sooner the better. Donna Sue's pregnancy hadn't started to show yet, but she was already thinking of working part-time.

Lacey had worked so hard to work her way through college, then law school, and now up the partnership ladder. She was almost there, so close she could envision it. From a quick glance at her company email, she would have plenty of opportunities to keep her on the right track. She had answered only the critical ones before B.J. asked for homework help. Otherwise Lacey would have been immersed in email for hours.

But she was discovering that she hadn't minded being pulled away from work for family. She felt just as fulfilled when she explained grammar to B.J. as she did when she saved her clients millions of dollars.

This time last week, Lacey would have dumped Donna Sue's idea in file thirteen and walked away without another thought. But today was different.

Donna Sue's offer meant much less financial success and fewer accolades. It also meant less hours, less stress, lower cost of living, and family just minutes away and living in the town she'd fought so hard to escape. And it meant being close to Hank.

The water turned cold and the bubbles began to pop, one at a time, and Lacey still hadn't made a decision.

Hank let the water beat down on his shoulders and hoped that the steam would loosen the knots that today's strain had made of his muscles.

Today's job had started out fantastic, but had ended up more nerve-wracking than the first time Hank had ever sprayed a field. After Lacey's visit, he'd spent the rest of the afternoon determined to concentrate strictly on his flying. But time after time Lacey's silly question about marriage had popped into his head when he should have been thinking of descent rate. He hadn't been this mentally exhausted since his first season, when he'd had to focus all his attention on each small detail of his flying.

He grabbed a pair of gym shorts to sleep in and made a mental note to buy shampoo next time at the grocery store.

A long yawn escaped. The day had been long and hard and tomorrow morning would come early.

He already knew he would love Lacey the rest of her life. Loving her as his wife took on a whole new meaning, and it didn't scare him nearly as much as he thought it would.

But they hadn't even said the L-word yet. If he begged on bended knee, what were the odds of Lacey agreeing to marry him? Slim to none? What about her job? What about his? Cropdusters weren't in big demand in downtown Chicago. And he still had Jennifer to worry about.

He turned off his bedroom light and slid into his cold bed. Outside, lightning flickered across the eastern sky and thunder rolled, deep and subtle.

Eminent thunderstorms fit Hank's mood perfectly.

Lacey stabbed around for the alarm's off button, trying to blink herself awake. After knocking her bedside clock to the floor, she realized that the ring had come from the phone, not the wounded clock.

In the distance, she heard Glenna's voice, too muffled to hear distinctly. Rain pattered against her windows, blocking out any sunshine that might have clued her in to what time it was.

She hung off the side of the bed and rescued her abused clock—10 A.M. She hadn't slept this late since she got the flu last fall. While she didn't feel achy, she did feel the need to burrow back under the covers. Maybe it was the rain making her feel dreary, or a backlash from nerves.

After all, a heck of a lot had happened since her vacation began last Friday afternoon and it was only Tuesday. With a groan, she pulled her pillow over her head, but hiding only made her feel claustrophobic. She might as well get up and see what the day would bring.

A microburst of rain beat against the window, as if it were a sign to stay inside, safe and dry. After a good night's sleep, she was coming back to her senses. She couldn't believe she'd even given any thought to Donna Sue's offer yesterday. She had put in years of study, of late hours, of missed opportunities for fun and friendship for her career. What was she thinking to even consider changing her life's goal so close to winning it?

The sooner she got this vacation over with, the sooner she could get back to life as normal. Seeing Hank, being around him, was bittersweet. Yes, she loved him from the bottom of her heart. No, she couldn't do anything about that love. Even if he felt the same way—he hadn't shown her any signs if he did—they lived in two different worlds.

She was disciplined and in control of her world. She would avoid thinking of Hank as anything more than a family friend and avoid further confusion. Her control only had to last for the next few days and then she would be back in Chicago, safe from the siren call of her small-town roots and safe from the one man who could knock her whole life off track.

As she rooted in the refrigerator for a diet Coke, Glenna joined her in the kitchen and dropped a kiss on her forehead. "You've been a popular young lady this morning. Donna Sue called and wants to have lunch tomorrow. And Hank called. Since he's weathered in, he's heading for the grocery store. He asked if you wanted to ride with him. I told him I'd have you call when you got up." Glenna handed Lacey a slip of paper torn from a used envelope. "I've made out a list, if you don't mind."

From memory, Lacey dialed Hank's number. At his deep, rich, "Hello" she felt her discipline falter. But strength of will had gotten her too far to fail her now.

In her most casual tone, she said, "Hey, I've got some

stuff to pick up too. I'll be ready in a half hour. Can you wait that long?"

"Sure. See you then."

Only after she hung up the phone did she realize she would be walking into the biggest gossip center in town. Well, who said life wouldn't have its little challenges?

Lacey climbed into Hank's truck and buckled up while he closed her door and settled into his own seat. She could blame her shivers on wearing shorts during a cool rainstorm, but the truth was that Hank didn't even have to brush against her to make her body react.

She must be becoming addicted to the electricity that kept the hairs on the back of her neck in a prickle whenever he was near, because her spirits picked up along with her pulse. But she had her trusty, tried-and-true plan.

Next week she would submerge herself in work to distract herself from the pain of withdrawal, and she would have the added bonus of being on top of the game, again.

The old, familiar back roads of West Monroe zipped by her window. Lacey felt like someone who'd once belonged here, but now could only look through the car window at what used to be. How many times had she vowed she would escape this little town?

After years of daydreams, nights filled with studying, and eons of hard work, she stood on the verge of success. The partnership beckoned, just beyond her fingertips. One more week and she'd attain the payoff she'd spent years sweating for.

Hank must have caught her mood, or be in one of his own, because he said nothing the whole trip in. Instead he devoted his attention to driving through the sparse traffic and fiddling with the radio. With her nerves on edge, Lacey wanted to slap his hand and tell him not to fidget. She twisted her fingers together, welcoming the ache in her knuckles, anything to divert the confusion in her heart.

Hank pulled into the grocery store parking lot, dodging a car that crossed his path. As soon as his truck's wheels stopped rolling Lacey escaped, intending to head for the refuge that heads of lettuce and rolls of toilet paper offered. She grabbed a shopping buggy and started past the checkout counter, not really caring which row she started on.

"Lacey Seivers? How good to see you. Don't you look good?" Rose Ann looked just like her mother used to, even to her oversized, dark-framed glasses. Rose Ann had been one of the meanest girls in high school. She had laughed at Lacey's awkwardness, had laughed at her clothes, and had laughed at her infatuation with Hank, no matter how many times Lacey had denied it back then.

Lacey tried to dodge, but she was too late. Rose Ann scooped Lacey into her arms, smothering her in Opium perfume, as she delivered the traditional Southern hug shared between old acquaintances. The pre-schooler attached to the end of Rose Ann's arm pushed and shoved in his effort to escape the three-way hug. His little hands left traces of something sticky on Lacey's bare calf.

Sneezing hard enough to break Rose Ann's hold, she

backed away, putting a buggy between them. "Good to see you, Rose Ann. You'll have to excuse me, but I've really got to get this shopping done."

Lacey whirled the buggy around and headed for refuge among the canned goods.

Rose Ann blocked her with a quick shove of her own buggy. "Your momma told me you'd be in town this week. I've been looking for you. Lots of folks are coming into town for the reunion. I heard you don't have a date for the dance, bless your heart. Do you want me to try to find you one?"

"No. I don't." Lacey didn't even try to keep the anger from her voice.

Rose Ann hadn't sweetened with age. Lacey tried to steer around Rose Ann but she tightened the space between a display of Granny Smith apples and her buggy, trapping Lacey.

"I hear that Jennifer Myers is in town for the reunion, and she asked for your phone number, Hank. Are you taking her to the dance?"

Hank propped his hand on Lacey's shoulder. "Lacey's going with me."

Even through the thickness of her glasses, Rose Ann turned predator's eyes on Hank, raking across him as if he were a piece of raw T-bone. "I hadn't heard that. You are such a nice man, Hank, knowing that with Lacey being out of town and all, she would have had a hard time finding a date for herself." She flashed a smile, as brilliant and as hard as diamonds, then her eyes slit like a cat's. "I'd heard something about you two at the ballpark the other night. So now you're taking Lacey to the dance, huh? I thought you weren't coming?"

Hank eased closer to Lacey's buggy, elbow to elbow. "When I had the opportunity to bring Lacey, I jumped at the chance."

"That's right. You're in business with her folks, aren't you? Making points with the boss?"

Lacey aimed her own barb. "How have you done for yourself, Rose Ann? I remember you had such big plans. Soap opera star, wasn't it?"

Hank wrapped his arms around Lacey, giving her a big bear hug. While Hank might think he was trying to comfort her, to Lacey that hug felt more like he was trying to hold her back. She wriggled to make him loosen his hold and tried to tell him through her glare that she didn't need a bodyguard. She'd been a survivor of more catfights than she could count.

Rose Ann must have learned a little something in the last ten years. Or maybe her survival instincts kicked in, because she had the sense to release the bar and allow her son to drag her back a step.

But she still had to get in the last sentence. She maneuvered her buggy in front of Lacey's to stop her and looked up at Hank. "I'm sure a big city lawyer like Lacey doesn't need to rely on a man to get her where she wants to go."

The words were right. It was the cotton candy tone, way too sugary to be sincere, but still not sweet enough to cover up the bitterness of sour grapes, that set Lacey's teeth on edge.

Hank unlocked the truck door for Lacey and loaded up the sack of bruised lettuce and tomatoes that Lacey had catapulted into her buggy, along with his own bare necessities of cereal, milk, and shampoo.

The sun was out for now, making the air heavy and thick outside. Hank cranked on the air conditioner but couldn't dissipate the heaviness inside the truck. Anger and tension weren't so easily blown away.

"I don't need a date to the dance." The quiet growl of her voice sent chills down Hank's spine.

He swallowed hard. "I could have done that a lot better. I'm sorry. But Jennifer will be there, it might be better if I went, too, to try to squash anything she might start. So, I was hoping, maybe, that you would . . ."

Lacey crossed her arms and let out a deep sigh. "All right, fine. I'll go with you. How could I turn down such a gracious invitation?"

He would have thanked her, begged forgiveness, offered to kiss the ground she walked on, but the set of Lacey's jaw didn't encourage further conversation. Instead he was stuck with his own torturous thoughts.

A sideways glance showed him Lacey's profile, brow furrowed and lips tight. He couldn't see her eyes behind her sunglasses, which was just has well. He could do without another look at those poison darts her eyes had been shooting.

Had it always been this way for Lacey, with mean-spirited kids taking potshots at her to make themselves feel better? He was learning, with Cody, that such petty behavior happened in all school groups but he'd never even noticed it until his own son started experiencing it. Had Lacey been the one in their school? He'd wondered why she stood apart from his group of friends in high school but then he'd been too conceited to think of anyone but himself. No wonder she shook the dust of West Monroe from her heels as soon as she was able.

Why would Lacey want to leave everything she had worked for in Chicago and come back to West Monroe?

He drove past the high school where they were hanging a *Welcome Alumni* banner across the entrance. Cheerleaders were leading a rally on the front lawn and an isolated knot of students stood under a tree watching, apart from the crowd.

Lacey would have been in that group while Jennifer would have been doing back flips and high kicks.

Jennifer.

Any complications about his and Lacey's future would have to wait. He had more immediate concerns.

What was he going to do about Jennifer? He'd put off his talk with Cody long enough.

Chapter Eleven

Hank waited on the front porch while Cody's bus pulled to a stop in his driveway.

His muscles quivered with the need to snatch up his son and hold him so tight that no one could ever get close enough to hurt him. Right now, he was having a hard time finding that line between protecting and suffocating.

"Aw, Dad, you're home. I thought I'd get to stay by myself today."

"I can't fly in this weather, son." Hank ran Glenna's lecture over and over through his mind about holding on too tight and losing your children altogether, until he found the courage to say, "Maybe tomorrow."

"I told everyone on the bus that I was staying by myself and now they'll say I made it up. If it rains tomorrow, could you stay inside and let me use my key to open the door?"

"I can probably do that." Hank held open the screen door for Cody. "Take your shoes off here on the steps, then get some dry socks on."

Cody headed down the hall, but called over his shoulder, "I'm hungry. What's to eat?"

As Hank searched his bare pantry, he thought of the nearly empty buggy he'd pushed through the cashier's line at the grocery store and got uptight all over again. This would be one heck of an afternoon.

When he heard Cody turn on the TV, he walked into the den, feeling a need to see his son, to reassure himself that Cody was all right.

Cody didn't even look up from the television. He hadn't been home over five minutes and he already had the den looking like a tornado hit it. His book bag spilled out across the couch. His shoes blocked the doorway to the hall, and his wet socks lay scattered across the rug.

"You want me to make brownies, Cody?"

"'Kay," Cody mumbled. He turned back to his TV show, forgetting about dear old dad before Hank even made it out of the room.

Hank measured and mixed and stalled for time. He had to talk to Cody about Jennifer, but where did he begin? No matter how hard he tried to think of an opening sentence, his mind wandered away.

If he and Cody left for Chicago, how long would it take Jennifer to figure out they'd moved? Was she even a concern, or like Lacey said, did she just want to make an appearance at the reunion and go back to wherever she came from?

How would Cody adjust to living in Chicago? They were both plain and simple country boys. How would Hank help his son get used to big city ways?

Hank wasn't even sure how *he* would make the transition and he wanted it all straight in his head before he talked it over with Lacey. He wanted to tell her what was in his heart, how much he loved her, what a great wife and mother she would be, and what a great husband he would try to be for her. He wanted to reassure Lacey that he would never expect her to give up the life she loved for him and Cody but he had to be sure he could give up his and Cody's instead. Right now, he wasn't sure about anything.

He certainly wasn't sure about how to get through this talk with Cody about his mother.

His fingers itched to call Lacey, to cry on her shoulder, to bury his head in her hair and stay there until the hurt went away. Even though she was angry at him, he knew she would talk him through this and maybe give him a place to start.

Lacey didn't know, would never know, how many times she'd saved his sanity. That one night a decade ago she had saved his life and hadn't even known it.

He'd been so young and so stupid and so scared that hellacious night he found out that Jennifer's "freshman fifteen" weight gain wasn't from too many calories drunk from the keg.

With no privacy at the frat house, he'd stumbled to a phone booth and used the whole roll of quarters he'd saved for that month's laundry to call Notre Dame. The phone receiver had smelled of old beer and cigarettes, and the phone had rung six times before Lacey picked up. If she hadn't answered, he still wasn't sure what he'd have done.

Even though his midnight call had awakened her, she said it didn't matter, she was always glad to hear from him. He told her he was getting married. Did she want to be his best man? And the godmother to his child? Then he had practiced popping the question on Lacey until he got the words in the right order.

Lacey had answered right every time. But then he'd really screwed up the delivery when he asked Jennifer the next morning and accidentally said Lacey's name instead of Jennifer's.

Jennifer's answer hadn't been a soft little yes, or even a soft little no. It was a raging, screaming, hysterical no. Everyone in her sorority house must have heard her. Within two hours, it was all over campus.

It was all Hank's fault, Jennifer had said. She did not want to be married, not to him, not to anyone. Married and pregnant did not fit into her future plans.

Then Jennifer delivered a month early, during finals week. She signed over all her rights to Hank while she was still in the hospital, stipulating he never try to contact her or her family. She wanted to put it all behind her, forget it ever happened and go on with her life. Two days later, she left for Dallas to model and had ended up as a Dallas Cowboys Cheerleader.

And Hank had sat with his premature infant son, willing the little guy to keep sucking in air. Every night

Lacey called—to see how the baby was to see how he was to ask if he'd called the adoption agency yet. And when he decided three weeks later that he couldn't give up his son, she had reassured him that he would be a wonderful father.

For the millionth time in five minutes, Hank wished Lacey could be with him, maybe even hold his hand as he talked with Cody. But there were some things a man had to do on his own.

He went into his bedroom to take a breath and steel his nerves. The answering machine on his business line blinked next to his bed.

Hank pushed the playback button on the answering machine.

As he listened to Donna Sue's message, he waffled between wishing he'd never seen the red blinking light and wishing he'd been here when she called.

"Hank, I got a visit from Jennifer Myers today. She wanted to hire me to advise her on Louisiana's custody laws. Of course I turned her down, since you and Billy already have me on retainer for your business. You probably need a lawyer for this one too, Hank."

Hank barely restrained himself from ripping the answering machine from the nightstand and throwing it against the wall—as if that would help.

How much worse could this day get?

The second the thought formed in Hank's head, he wished he could take it back. Whenever he thought he had hit bottom, things always got worse.

It took a while for Hank to realize that the roar in his

ears wasn't his blood pressure rising but the buzzing of the oven timer.

As he pulled the hot pan from the oven, Cody skated toward the table, his dry socks sliding on the polished wood floor. "Hey Dad, I smell the brownies. Are there any that aren't burnt?"

"I salvaged a few. Wash your hands and help yourself."

"Cool." Cody scrubbed away a layer of dirt, glancing back over his shoulder at his father. With a dragging voice, Cody said, "Dad, there's something I gotta talk to you about."

Hank's stomach sank as he looked at his son's woebegone eyes. "I'm all ears."

Hank trimmed off the overcooked edges from the brownies and put the rest on a plate. They didn't look or smell as good as Lacey's but they'd have to do. As if it mattered. He couldn't put one in his mouth and swallow it right now, if his life depended on it.

"You know that math test I had today? Well, I didn't do very well. I didn't even get to finish. I only finished the ones like Lacey helped me with. Do you think she could help me with my homework this week?"

Math test? Hank released his pent-up breath. Funny how the important things in life put math tests into perspective. "We'll ask her. And don't worry too much about the test. I know you studied and did your best."

Behind his glasses, Cody raised his eyebrows in astonishment. Then he accepted his good fortune with a shrug of his shoulders. "I'll try harder next time."

"I know you will, son." Hank ran his hand over his

son's hair as Cody seated himself at the kitchen table. The boy filled his mouth full of brownies and made an appreciative groan. "These are good, Dad. Did you use Lacey's recipe?"

"As a matter of fact, I did." Hank sat at the table, reached for a brownie, then drew his hand back. Trying to eat anything right now would be like trying to eat sawdust. "I'm taking Lacey to my high school reunion dance."

"Yeah? Cool! Winnie said that Jennifer Meyers would be there too. Somebody brought an old magazine with her picture in it." Cody stopped chewing and stared at Hank. "Winnie says that you used to date Jennifer Myers."

A day late and a dollar short just about summed up Hank's life. "Winnie's right. I did date her all through high school and my first year at college."

"Winnie said you dated lots of girls."

Hank twitched in his chair while Cody pinned him with an unblinking stare. "I went out with a few different women, but mostly I dated Jennifer."

"She's my mother, isn't she?" Cody crumbled the brownie in his plate. Then he traced through the crumbs with his fingers. "Jennifer Meyers is my mom."

Hank choked out the answer. "Yes, Cody. Jennifer is your mother."

"Why did she leave?"

How many times had Hank asked himself that same question?

"She was young, too young to be a good mother." As

Hank said the words, a tight band loosened around his heart. She *had* been too young. He had always felt she had betrayed Cody by leaving him. Today Hank felt an inkling of sympathy for the scared, confused girl she had been. "Even though she didn't stay in our lives, I'll always be grateful that she gave me you."

"Really, Dad? You didn't just keep me because nobody else wanted me?" A tear tracked down Cody's cheek, pooling in the corner of his mouth. How could Hank make his son understand?

"I kept you because I couldn't have lived without you, son." Hank felt his own eyes brim over. He resisted the urge to wipe at his face. If his son could be man enough to cry, then so could he. "Several families wanted to adopt you, but I couldn't let you go. It was a selfish decision, but it was the only one I could make."

For the first time in ages, Hank opened his arms and gathered Cody into his lap. He nestled his cheek against his son's soft, blond hair, remembering the sweet baby smell from years ago. "I've never regretted my decision for a single minute. You are the best thing that ever happened to me."

Cody rested his head against his father's chest, and Hank had never known such peaceful fulfillment.

"Dad? I've got a question. You aren't going to let her take me away from you, are you?"

Hank tried to keep the tension from his voice. "No one and nothing will take you away from me."

"That's good, Dad. Because when she tried to check

me out at school today, Mr. Welsh said she had to have your permission and she said she'd just see about that."

Hank felt like he'd been shoved off a ten-story building, and he hadn't even known he'd been standing close to the edge.

Cody squirmed. "Dad, you're squishing me."

"Sorry, son." Hank loosened his hold. "Why didn't you tell me this when you first came in the door?"

"I didn't want to upset you. Besides, I knew you wouldn't let her take me." Cody looked up with Jennifer's sky-blue eyes. "She's pretty, isn't she?"

Hank swallowed down all he wanted to say, for his son's sake. "She's beautiful."

Cody hopped down from Hank's lap. "She's not as pretty as Lacey, though."

"I'd have to agree with you on that one." Hank scraped brownie crumbs into the palm of his hand. "When it comes to good looks, our Lacey's got everyone beat."

"Is Lacey a better kisser?"

Best kisses I've ever had. Hank frowned down at Cody. "A gentleman never kisses and tells."

"Let's call her about this math homework, okay?"

Hank wanted to say yes, his mouth even formed the words. "No, I'll help you." Right now, with his head in a whirl, he couldn't share his son, not even with Lacey.

Five math problems later, he wished he hadn't been so hasty. They had struggled through them, Cody and he, like they'd struggled through many other times. But having Lacey around would have made this homework session easier and not only because she understood this stuff. He'd always taken for granted that when Lacey entered a room, she brought her own personal sunbeam along.

As he scooped up the last paper wad from the kitchen floor, the phone began to ring. He really needed to hear Lacey's voice right now.

Cody looked up from snapping his smudged homework sheet into his notebook. "Aren't you going to answer that?"

"Sure, son." He hoped it was Lacey, but what were the odds? It could be anyone. It could be Jennifer. "Hello?"

"Hank? It's Lacey." Of course, it was. As if he wouldn't recognize her voice. As if he hadn't known it would be her, calling to make sure he was okay. How did she always know when he needed her?

"Hey Lacey, what's up." The words were cheerful for Cody's sake, even if he couldn't make his tone match.

"B.J. told me that Jennifer showed up at school today. Is Cody okay?"

"Yeah, fine. He's standing right next to me."

"How are you?"

"Can you come over?"

"I'm on my way."

With Cody mesmerized by the TV inside, Lacey sat on the tailgate of Hank's truck while he paced, then sat, then paced again. She folded up the crinkled custody papers and put them back into the envelope. "You're right, it's a tight agreement. You can't contact her and neither can anyone working on your behalf. That would dissolve the agreement."

"Why did she go to his school and scare him like that? Why didn't she come to me first?"

"I imagine she will. You don't want to hear this, but when she does get in touch with you, have you thought about letting her see Cody? If you make some kind of compromise offer like supervised visits you might be able to come to an agreement."

"She left us, left him. I've been the parent Cody has always looked to for protection, for explanations, for love. What if she wants Cody to live with her? What if she drops into his life long enough to make him care, then decides to drop out again?"

Is that what she did to you? Now wasn't the time to ask. Now they needed to focus on Cody. But then, she didn't really need to ask. The pain in his voice said it all.

"It's been a long time since I studied family law. Corporate's a whole different world. I did a little research today and the only thing consistent about Louisiana custody laws is that each case is different. If you don't reach an agreement outside of court, a judge's order could be much worse. Do you want to take that chance?"

"How much of a chance is it?"

"I don't know. Nobody knows. It depends on which social worker is assigned to your case, which judge you draw, and how much you and Jennifer are willing to rip each other to shreds while Cody stands by and watches."

"Social workers? Tell me what I can expect."

"If Jennifer does want custody—and we don't know

yet that she does—she could ask for different judgments. She can ask for visitation rights, or shared custody, or even total custody with child support."

"And she could get it?"

"From the cases I glanced at, maybe. She can say she was too young and emotional to make the decision to sign that agreement. She can get her parents involved and ask for grandparents' rights. She can even try to prove you're an incompetent parent."

Lacey's heart broke as Hank buried his face in his hands. "When I first brought him home, I used to have bad dreams about her showing up and taking Cody away from me. I'd wake up sweating and end up sleeping on the floor next to his crib. But the real thing is worse than all those nightmares put together." He scrubbed the back of his hand across his red-rimmed eyes. "In those cases you read, what was the worse outcome?"

"I only had time to finish one. The two parents came to an agreement and settled out of court."

"What was the agreement?"

"They married each other."

The rumble of thunder in the distance warned of another rainy night. "I'm already behind schedule. If these storms don't blow over tonight and I miss tomorrow's flights, I'll have to let Cody spend the night with your folks the rest of the week so I can leave the house early. I'll have to max out my hours and fly from dawn to dusk. Probably all day Sunday, too. That's the kind of information Jennifer would use against me, isn't it?"

"Yeah, that's what she would be looking for." Lacey

brushed grit from her hands. "Maybe you could reschedule?"

"Any other week but this one. I squeezed in a job that I probably shouldn't have. Glenna warned me, but I didn't want to turn down that new customer in Bastrop, so I squeezed him in Saturday morning. With the dance Saturday night, I've got to be in early enough to clean up."

"I'm a big girl. You don't have to take me to the dance if you don't want to."

Yeah, that would be the thing. To make Lacey go to that reunion dance alone so all those hens could peck at her. "I *want* to take you. Besides, I've already put down a deposit on the tux."

"Oh, well, that settles it, then."

He couldn't even summon a grin for Lacey's gentle teasing.

The screen door screeched and Cody leaned out, "Dad, are you gonna come inside soon? You said we'd read another chapter together before bed."

"Sure, son. I'll be right there." After Cody went back inside, Hank sat and looked up at the sky with blank eyes. Lightning streaked in the distance, mesmerizing him. He didn't even notice when Lacey started the trek home alone.

"Dad? Why are you sitting out there by yourself?"

Hank shook himself out of his dive into bleakness and faked a light tone. "I'm just enjoying the peace and quiet."

"Where did Lacey go? You didn't kiss her again, did you?"

No, he hadn't. But he wished he had. When their lips met, he could think of nothing else. What would Lacey think of being the world's best anesthesia? What did *he* think of her being so much more?

Hank read until Cody dropped off to sleep, then turned off the light and brushed the hair off his forehead.

He couldn't make himself go. He just sat beside his son's bed listening to him breathe.

Chapter Twelve

From the moment she woke up the weather had been iffy, with tall white clouds rolling across the sun, casting shadows and making her shiver.

Late afternoon found Lacey sitting cross-legged on the floor in front of the TV, watching a silly talk show and playing Solitaire while trying to digest Donna Sue's offer. Although the rain hadn't started yet, the thunderclouds darkened the living room that had been bright enough an hour ago. Lightning popped, sounding closer than it had minutes earlier.

Despite the bad weather, Lacey felt unusually comfortable and content, like a round peg that had finally found her circular hole after too many years trying to fit into the square one.

She should have been reading her office email, had been trying to convince herself to dial up the Internet for the last hour, but couldn't bring herself to check on her corporate responsibilities while she nestled among her family. Thunder rumbled and the lights blinked, giving Lacey the excuse she needed to avoid going on-line. What if lightning zapped the phone system and she lost her modem?

Halfway through another game of Solitaire, the skies darkened enough that Lacey had to turn the lights on to see. Flashes of lightning strobed across the sky, followed by crashes of thunder. Lacey counted four seconds between the strikes and the rumbles, much closer than a few minutes ago.

The phone rang and Lacey leaned over to grab the portable receiver.

"Lacey, this is Hank."

"I can barely hear you."

"Yeah, this wind is pretty bad. Listen, I'm running behind and I don't want Cody by himself at the house today. Could you get him off the bus with B.J. and keep him at your place until I get home? I'll come over and get him as soon as I touch down. He won't be too happy that he's not getting to stay by himself, but he'll have to get over it."

"Sure. Just be careful."

"Yeah, great. . . . can barely hear . . ." The rumble of thunder overpowered most of Hank's words and Lacey strained to understand bits and pieces. ". . . Billy . . . open the barn door. . . . weather . . . hard and fast . . . taxi in quick."

"Sure." Lacey flinched as lightning crackled over the phone. "Hank. Be careful."

"Always."

The phone went silent while the wind howled, making the screen door bang. Lightning cracked, turning the living room into black-and-white. The thunder boomed as the strike flickered. A gust of wind whipped the pillows from the porch rocking chairs and made the swing creak on its chains.

Glenna came in, lighting candles and an oil lantern. "I don't know how much longer we'll keep our lights on. Who was on the phone, dear?"

"That was Hank. When the bus gets here, we need to get Cody off with Beej. I need to run over and open the barn doors for him, too."

Glenna lost all color in her face. "He's not flying in this, is he? Zeb's got my car so you'll have to take his truck. And take my cell phone. It'll work even if the lights go out. Call and let me know when Hank touches down."

"I will."

Glenna's fear fed her own until Lacey was nauseated with worry. She alternated between watching for the bus and watching the storm.

Lacey herded both B.J. and Cody off the bus and into the Seivers' kitchen, where her mom waited with milk and cookies. She rushed for Zeb's truck and headed for Hank's. Leaves skittered across the road in front of her and limbs bent and swayed, threatening to break.

She drove around back to the barn, parking as close to the doors as she could. Bolt after bolt of lightning cracked. The sharp crashes rolled into deep continuous thunder that settled heavily in her stomach. As the lightning flickered, she searched the skies but couldn't find the black speck of a plane against the dark clouds.

The first fat drop splashed her face as she worked the barn door latch free. By the time she pushed open the heavy wooden doors, she was soaked through. Lacey turned on every overhead light in the barn, including the one in the loft.

Where was Hank? His plane was small and fabric, not made for flying through thunderstorms. Although she listened for his motor, all she heard was the storm. In a corner filled with tarps and old quilts, Lacey settled in to bite her fingernails and wait.

Using the barn light as a beacon, Hank touched down on the slick grass landing strip that he couldn't see but experience told him was there. He'd always said he could fly home blind, but had never imagined that he'd have to prove it. He taxied down the strip and into the open barn.

As he climbed out of the cockpit, he allowed his hands to shake and his knees to quiver. Two deep breaths and he reined in his nerves to make his legs solid enough to walk on.

How could he have been so stupid? The spring storm, filled with microbursts, almost won this time. Would it have hurt to spend the night in Bastrop? The farmer had even offered him a warm bed.

But, no, Mr. Superpilot had to chance the weather and fly home. He could've had Cody spend the night with the Seivers, but he had wanted to be home with his son. He had wanted to reassure Cody that he wasn't deprived because he didn't have a mother. Instead he had almost deprived Cody of a father as well.

Life was so fragile.

Lacey was right. Cody was entitled to know his mother if she was willing to know him. A boy couldn't have too much love in his life. But she would never take Cody from him.

An involuntary shiver skittered down Hank's spine. Thoughts of sharing were hard enough. He could never let Cody go. Despite the muggy one-hundred-degree day, Hank felt cold to the marrow of his bones. He closed his eyes and gathered his strength.

A rustling sound disturbed his meditation. He looked into the shadows and saw Lacey. "What are you doing out here? You're soaked. You could have waited at the house."

Lacey pushed away from the dark corner she had been leaning against and walked toward him just like in his dreams.

"Welcome home, flyboy." She looked up at him through the droplets spiking her eyelashes.

A strand of hair lay across her forehead near her eyebrow. He reached out and tucked it behind her ear.

She turned her head and kissed the tips of his fingers. "I was so worried."

He tilted up her head. Lacey's mouth tasted warm and full. *Good heavens, what am I doing?*

He started to pull away, but Lacey entwined her hands

around the back of his head and pulled him closer. His mood changed from brooding to bliss.

He lifted her chin and guided her mouth to his.

At first her kiss was tender and seeking. "I was so scared," she whispered. Her kiss intensified, revealing all her emotions.

"Beautiful. You're so beautiful it hurts." Dazed, he looked into her eyes. "Lacey, I love you."

She wrapped her arms around his shoulders and pulled him to her so tight he could feel her heart beat next to his. "I love you too, Hank."

Her knees buckled but Hank held her close. "Oh, Hank, I can't stand on my own two feet anymore."

Gently he guided them down to the mound of quilts with Lacey's head cradled on his shoulder and her fingers intertwined with his. Against his ribs, he could feel her heartbeat in counterpoint to his own. It was the harmony he'd needed all his life. Lacey made his blood sing, made his heart race, and then soothed him into tranquility.

Outside the barn, rain fell, strong and steady, louder than the thunder rumbling in the distance. A warm breeze carried in the clean, wet smell of grass and trees but nature's perfume couldn't compete with the fragrance of Lacey—all woman and all his.

She gazed at him with such love he felt humbled by her. Her hair hung over her shoulders, her eyes looked sultry and deep, her lips soft and full. Using every ounce of willpower he owned, he pushed away from her.

He folded her hand in his and knelt on one knee.

He wrapped his arms around her so she couldn't see

his face, but she heard the pain in his voice. "I'm not good with words, but there's this empty place inside me, like a big hole or a bottomless well. That place stays cold and dark, and I'm afraid that the part of me that's missing makes me not enough. Except when I'm with you, I don't feel that way at all. Whenever you're around, or even if I just think about you, that hole fills with light and warmth, and I feel like I'm a good man, a worthy man who has something to give. I love you, Lacey. Will you marry me?"

She wanted to say yes, opened her mouth and wet her lips intending to say yes. But she couldn't. Not yet.

All the dreams she'd had of this moment had been fantasies and illusions. Marriage to Hank would be real, day in and day out. Car notes and garbage day and ready-made motherhood. This would be for keeps. She had to search her own soul and make sure she could give everything to marriage that Hank and Cody would deserve from her. "There's so much between us, Hank. So much unsettled."

"Don't worry about your job. Cody and I will move to Chicago. It might take a while to find your parents another partner and I'll need to stay here until then, but it'll probably take a while to find a bigger place there anyway, right?" Hank's words ran together, his voice cracking with worry. He was willing to give up his career, his whole way of life for her?

That made her answer ever harder. "I have to think about it. There's more than just the two of us to consider. You've got a lot going on in your life right now.

You don't need any more complications. And I don't need to make a hasty decision."

Slowly, Hank climbed to his feet, but kept hold of her hand. "But you love me, right?"

"More than anyone else on earth."

He rubbed his cheek against her hair, then released her. Immediately, she felt anchorless, adrift, and lonely.

He walked to the barn door and stared out at the setting sun. "Tell Cody he can spend the night if he wants to."

Lacey's throat closed until she couldn't breathe. She closed her eyes and drew in a deep breath. "Okay."

As she walked out to the truck, she couldn't help glancing back at Hank. He leaned against the barn door, feet braced, head back, and eyes closed.

He looked so alone.

Chapter Thirteen

For the last three days, Lacey had seen a lot of Cody but nothing of his father. She understood that it was Hank's busy time of year with the threat of spring rains making every hour in the air critical to his bottom line, but still, she missed him more every minute. She made a point to wake up early to hear his plane take flight in the pre-dawn hours and to send up a plea for his safety before she helped her mom get the boys off to school.

True to his promise, he'd been letting Cody stay home by himself but he'd been cutting his day short, never leaving Cody alone for more than a half hour.

To make up for his early quitting time, Hank was leaving out earlier. Instead of waking his son and sending him to the Seivers before the stars even faded, he would feed Cody supper, listen to his day and then send him to Glenna and Billy's for bed so Cody could get

179

enough sleep. From what Pop said, missing those extra hours of sleep was taking a toll on Hank, but even worse, missing mornings with his son was breaking Hank's heart.

Lacey could have called to chat or even walk over but Hank had too little time with his son as it was. She wouldn't interfere. And he hadn't tried to contact her either.

She filled her days with whatever made her happy, helping Pop in the shop, indulging in naps in the afternoons, and helping with supper and homework in the evenings.

She had thought long and hard about her life. Yes, she had almost reached her goal, but had it brought her joy?

Pride? Yes. Satisfaction? Definitely. But joy?

At first, she had thrived on the fast pace, the long hours, and the thrill of negotiating with the big boys. But now when she thought of all those intense hours, she only felt drained. When she made partner, those demands would be worse. Bragging rights and big paychecks weren't enough compensation for a lifestyle that didn't bring her joy.

Being with her family in West Monroe gave her serenity, but that wasn't enough. Hearing Hank's footsteps when he came in the door gave her joy. Watching Cody's face when he ate her brownies gave her joy.

And joy was more than enough reason to give up her goal of becoming a successful partner in one of Chicago's biggest law firms.

Donna Sue had been delighted yesterday when Lacey

agreed, and she began paperwork for their partnership. It would take a few months to make the transition, plenty of time to tie up loose ends in Chicago.

Wow, what a week!

Thank heavens tomorrow was Saturday. Not only would she see Hank again, she would see him at her best. Her dress really was killer. She would hold her own against any woman there, including Jennifer.

She wondered when Hank would find the note she had left on his nightstand.

Hank unlocked the door and stumbled in, his headache so bad his vision was blurry. The last three days had been hell. It had taken all his willpower to give Lacey the space she needed.

The house was dark and lonely without Cody. The Seivers had scooped him up and taken him to the ballpark with a promise of pizza afterward.

Hank took two aspirin and headed for bed, knowing he wouldn't sleep but hoping he could rest enough to fly adequately in the morning. He didn't even bother to turn on the light, but lay down, clothes and all.

Visions of a future full of Lacey flooded his imagination and his whole house felt too big and empty without her.

He glanced at the clock and that's when he saw the answering machine's blinking red light.

The call could be from anyone, a farmer unhappy with the delayed schedule, a parent-teacher meeting, or maybe even Lacey.

There were some voices you never forgot.

Jennifer Myers' was one of them. It was still raspy and ultrafeminine, and it still sent shivers down his spine. But the shivers were from dread, not from passion.

The tape reached the end and Hank realized he would have to replay the message. He didn't remember a word she had said.

"Hank, this is Jennifer. It's been a while, hasn't it? I'd like to talk to you—alone. Call me."

Twice more he hit replay to scribble down the phone number. Still, as shaky as his hands were, he hoped he could read the number in the morning.

Then he noticed the paper he had written on. In Lacey's handwriting, the note said "I'm done with thinking about it."

Lacey's morning went by in a blur, with last minute fittings for the night ahead and a few chores to make the time pass.

Shortly after noon, while she was loading the dishwasher, she heard Hank's plane fly in. She knew he'd planned a short day because of the dance tonight, but thought he'd meant early afternoon, not just after lunch.

She couldn't seem to control her frequent glances at the phone. She'd give him thirty minutes then she'd call him.

But just five minutes passed before she saw his truck head into town.

Intently, Lacey scrubbed a sticky spot with her fingernail. He could be heading in early to pick up his tux or for any number of other reasons, maybe even flowers.

"Honey, did you get shoes yet? You don't want to wear this old pair of mine, I'm sure." Glenna's unexpected appearance startled Lacey, and she broke her nail against the counter.

Running her finger over the ragged edge, she studied the shoes her mom held. "I guess I should go shopping, huh? Maybe I should stop in for a manicure too."

"Good idea, sweetie. Take your time and enjoy yourself. That's what vacations are for."

The more Lacey thought about her shopping trip, the more the idea appealed to her. Lacey snagged the keys to her mom's car and headed into town.

Soon this fifteen-minute trip into town would be an everyday occurrence. The commute might be a bit longer than the stroll down the sidewalk from her Chicago apartment to her old job, but the scenery couldn't be beat.

In Chicago, her view had been concrete streets, bordered by concrete sidewalks, running alongside concrete buildings.

Now, she drove past framed farmhouses set on sprawling, wildflower-covered pastureland. Closer into town, the rambling acreage gave way to brick ranch-styles or deeply porched Arcadian houses with manicured lawns and beds of spring annuals. With all the rain, the ornamental pears bloomed fluffy white against the new green leaves. Redbirds, sparrows, and an occasional bluebird flew from bush to tree, looking for worms and insects.

She slowed as she neared the banks of the Ouachita River and the trail to The Point. From the road, even in broad daylight, she couldn't see the spot where Hank and she had spent the night. On a whim, she parked beside the deeply rutted dirt road toward the river and walked toward the clearing that would forever have a special place in her heart.

And saw Hank's truck under the same tree where he had parked with her. But this time the woman walking with him along the riverfront was Jennifer.

Jennifer Myers Stanford stared absently at the river as she twisted her new wedding band around her finger.

It wasn't the worn jeans or the simple blue T-shirt, it was the ring that showed Hank how much she changed more than anything else. A simple, plain band of shiny gold and not even a diamond engagement ring to accompany it.

She'd wanted to walk, and Hank was grateful for the action. Sitting still with Jennifer inside the close confines of his truck would have only made a bad situation worse.

After her initial, hesitant hello, Jennifer had yet to really look at him. Instead, she studied the flotsam on the river while Hank studied her and waited.

Twice her voice broke and she coughed to clear her throat. Finally, she turned her back on the river and faced him, but her focus skittered away and she ended up looking down at her mud-stained loafers.

"I'm sorry, Hank. It's not enough, but it's all I've got.

I'm sorry I tried to see Cody at school. I'm sorry I never called. I'm sorry I left you with all the responsibility." She blinked through the tears welling in her eyes. "When I told my husband that I'd tried to see Cody, he gave me a ten-minute lecture over the phone. I still don't think before I act sometimes. I've thought about trying to force you to let me see him. Steve tried to talk sense into me, but I wouldn't listen, not until I saw the truth of his words with my own eyes."

Jennifer paused, as if expecting Hank to say something, but there was no way he'd make this easy for her.

Finally she coughed to clear her throat of emotion. "I've checked around and everyone in town thinks you're a great parent and Cody hasn't lacked for anything, especially love. If you don't want me in Cody's life, I won't cause problems. I'll just leave town right now and that will be the end of it. But if you would let me see Cody, just every now and then, like an aunt or something, Hank, I would be so very careful with him."

Hank thought he'd been prepared for anything she might say, but her apologies caught him by surprise. He swallowed, tried to respond, but words wouldn't form. Thoughts wouldn't even form.

Jennifer took his hands in hers, looked into his eyes with unflinching courage, and waited for his judgment.

Who was he to judge? He tried to speak, but his throat convulsed. He swallowed, determined to say what he'd kept bottled up for a decade. "I've been mad at you for so long. Angry that you walked out on me, walked out on our son, walked out on the future I used to dream about for us. But reality would have been pretty grim, with us barely making ends meet, hating each other and hating ourselves. I would say that we were both too young, but I'm not sure age has anything to do with it. Maturity, though, that's another matter." He rubbed her hand along his check, then brought it to his lips. "Sometimes, when I stopped being mad at you, I thought you might have made the better choice to let him go. Maybe I was the selfish one. Maybe he'd have had better parents if I'd have let him go too."

She smiled and her eyes shined through her tears, the same way they used to shine after a big game. Back then her smile could light up a night game during a new moon.

The whole time she'd been pregnant, she'd never even cracked a grin.

He was grateful she'd found her smile again.

She stuck her hands in her jeans pockets. "Now you're just fishing for compliments. I've done a bit of snooping and everyone agrees that you're the world's best father. Cody's been lucky. And when you find the right woman to be his mother, he'll be the luckiest little boy alive."

"He already is."

Jennifer stooped down to pick up a rock and throw it into the river. The circles grew wider and wider until they washed into the riverbank. "I always thought you and Lacey should be together."

Hank followed the flight of a crane, clumsily flapping

from the bank to a sandbar. "Yeah? Why didn't you clue me in sooner?"

"Would you have listened?"

Hank considered her question. "No. I've never been too good at listening, but I'm getting better."

"I guess we both are."

Chapter Fourteen

With four hours before the dance, Lacey hunted for things to keep her busy. Things to keep her from thinking about how Jennifer and Hank used to get cozy down by The Point. Things to keep reminding her that, from now on, *she* would be the only woman that Hank would be cozy with down by The Point or anywhere else. Things to remind her that Hank really meant it when he said he loved her.

Too twitchy to sit for a manicure, she'd checked out the little boys section of the department store, wondering if Cody needed new socks. Then she'd checked out the china department and sporting goods too. After staring blankly at a row of neon-colored bait, she had finally wandered into a mega-shoe store.

Amidst cheerful, watered-down department store music, Lacey jammed another shoe over her foot, then jerked it off and let it fall into the pile surrounding her stool.

She deliberately replaced mental pictures of Jennifer and Hank at the riverfront with memories of Hank pointing out the butterflies, brushing her hair from her cheek, resting his head on her shoulder.

Hank loved her. He said he did. She wasn't second best. She was first choice. Any insecurities that she had were of her own making and not because she didn't trust Hank.

He had a darned good reason for being in their special place—with Jennifer. Hadn't *she* been the one who encouraged Hank to talk to Jennifer? She just wished he'd have picked a different place for their talk.

"I'm afraid that's all the stiletto heels we have in your size." The beleaguered salesclerk shrugged an apology, then knelt to reshelf two dozen shoes.

Lacey looked around at the mess she'd made. At least this one could be cleaned up.

She loved Hank. He loved her. End of story. She'd not create another mess between her and Hank, one that couldn't be straightened up as easily as this one. "I'll take these."

Lacey didn't blame the salesclerk for his deep sigh as he handed her the box from the first pair she'd tried on.

All the way home, she replayed, over and over, the tender moments she and Hank had shared.

It didn't matter that Hank was having an intimate conversation with Jennifer. What mattered was the look on Hank's face as he kissed her, the private tone of voice he used only with her when he told her how beautiful she was, the treasured way she felt when he touched her. What mattered was that he loved her and she loved him.

Once home, she set about making herself useful.

"Lacey!" Glenna yelled to get her attention over the vacuum.

Lacey flipped off the switch and listened to the *whir* fade to silence. "Did you want something?"

"I want you to quit cleaning my house. I may not be the world's best housekeeper, but it's clean enough." Glenna kissed her on the forehead to soften her half-teasing words.

"I was just keeping busy."

"I've got something better for you to do." Glenna shoved a cardboard box at her. "I don't do this for just anybody, but you *are* my daughter and a mother must sacrifice."

Lacey looked into the open box and found four shiny, new romance novels. "Wow, I get first pick?"

Glenna nodded and pointed to the bathroom. "Now go fix a big tub of bubbles and relax. But don't drop my new books into the tub."

She picked through the books and chose the one that had a cover model who looked almost like Hank. "Thanks, Mom."

Lacey usually bought her books at the corner book-store, but she'd have to remember to get a subscription when she settled into Hank's house—her house. Her heart skipped a happy beat as she thought about forever.

"If I knew those books would put such a smile on

your face, I'd have lent you a dozen of them a week ago. Now go, before your brothers jump in there first."

The warning did its job and Lacey raced to get her bubble bath. The books must have been just what Lacey needed because she was so engrossed in the story she didn't realize that the water was cold and her toes were wrinkled until Josh pounded on the door.

"If you don't come out, I'll take the hinges off."

"Give me five more minutes." Lacey toweled off, her shoulders free of tension.

"Hank stopped by for Cody and took B.J. with him too. He says he'll pick you up at seven for dinner before the dance."

So much for tension-free. She still had a two-hour wait.

That's when she realized that she had spent her whole life waiting for Hank. Grown-up Lacey made her own way in the world.

Hastily, Lacey shoved her arms through her robe sleeves, ignoring that they stuck to her wet skin. Hank had promised her a lovely dinner before the dance. That's when she had intended to promise him love without end, amen.

While a proposal over a glass of wine sounded romantic enough, she was growing rather fond of Hank's barn.

She took the portable phone and headed to her bedroom for privacy.

When Hank answered, she barely gave him time to say hello.

"Meet me in the barn, half an hour."

She twisted her hair up, took extra time with her mascara wand, and slipped into her dress and new shoes.

She inspected herself in the mirror. *Not too shabby, not too shabby at all.*

Her heels clipped down the hallway as she made her way to the kitchen key rack.

"Oh wow, sis!" Zeb was loud enough that the whole family gathered to look.

Pop took the sucker from his mouth. "Either I need to ride shotgun or you need those mechanic's overalls after all, baby girl."

Glenna elbowed him and Josh too, before he could add his say.

"Lovely, sweetie, just lovely." Her mother beamed and aimed her camera.

"Later, Mom." Lacey grabbed the tractor keys. "Gotta go."

On her heels, she minced her way through the grass but finally had to kick off her shoes to work the clutch.

The tractor moved at a crawl, but this time Lacey didn't mind the slow speed. Anticipation made the coming scene so much sweeter.

As she pulled around to Hank's barn, she saw him waiting with the doors open. Before the motor noise died, he gathered her in his arms and lifted her from the tractor seat.

"You've already asked me once, so I guess it's only fair that I ask you this time. Henry Aaron Chandler, will you marry me?"

His throat convulsed a couple of times and he choked out a strangled, "Yes."

She threw herself into his arms and covered his lips with hers, not giving him a chance to say anything else.

He wrapped his arms around her and captured her breath with his mouth. Lacey filled his heart, his soul, his every cell, until his whole universe was only Lacey.

"Lacey, honey." His lips moved against her throat.

"Hank?"

Calling on his last bit of resolve, he spoke into the hollow of her throat. "Lacey, honey, I've got to stop. This is killing me."

She cupped his face with her hands, capturing him. Her lashes fluttered over dazed, moss-green eyes, blinking reality back into focus. Once, twice, she swallowed. Then she pulled away from him, carefully clasped her hands in her lap, and stared at her clenched fingers. "I was hoping you'd be the easy one. Now for the hard sell."

"What?" He opened his eyes and searched hers.

"Cody." She rubbed her hands along her dress. "I'm not just becoming your wife, Hank, I'm becoming your son's mother too."

"I'll make it work."

"No, we'll make it work." She looked toward the house. "I love your son. I hope that someday he'll love me too."

Could any woman other than Lacey have a bigger

heart? "How could he keep from it? You're going to be such a terrific mom."

He couldn't keep away from her. Just one more kiss.

As he nuzzled her neck, she whispered in his ear, "I'm glad you think so. Did I mention that I want babies? Lots of your babies."

He remembered how the emotions had welled up in him the first time Cody had wrapped his tiny hand around Hank's finger.

Cody had always been enough for Hank, more than enough some days, but he wouldn't mind having a little green-eyed girl, or maybe another boy, since he'd had a bit of practice now.

He would watch her belly become gently rounded then full with his child. He would massage Lacey's back when it ached. Her feet too, if she wanted him to. He would rest his hand on her stomach and feel his baby kick. All the things he had missed the first time around.

Making babies with Lacey would be a perfect way to spend his life.

"Is that your cell phone ringing?" Lacey's voice was so sultry, so sexy, it took a while for Hank to realize what she'd said.

"That's probably Cody calling. I'd better answer it." Parental duty had him reluctantly rolling away from Lacey's outstretched arms. Immediately he felt the chill, inside and out.

Digging for the phone, Hank found it on the seventh ring. Whoever called him was darned persistent. The caller ID confirmed that Cody was calling him from the house. "What's up, son?"

"We're hungry. What are you and Lacey doing out there anyway?"

For obvious reasons, discussions of future babies would have to wait.

Lacey slipped on one of Hank's button-down shirts and rolled the sleeves to her elbows to protect her dress. In the kitchen, she poked through the refrigerator and the pantry, planning supper for the boys, while Hank supervised Cody and B.J.'s clean-up efforts, a result of the boys' popcorn fight that had spread throughout the house.

The roar of the vacuum cleaner grew more muffled as Cody and B.J. pushed it down the hall into Cody's room. Since they played while they cleaned, the boys would be busy for a while.

This felt good. It felt right. It felt like what she wanted from her life.

As she thawed the chicken breasts in the microwave, she made her decision. "Hank? When you get a chance, we need to talk."

Immediately, she heard his footsteps from the living room. "Is this a good talk or a bad one? Wait, don't answer yet." Then he stood behind her, brushing her hair to the side, kissing her neck and making her shiver. "Okay, now talk."

With Hank nibbling at her ear, Lacey couldn't stammer out a single sentence. She staggered to a chair at the kitchen table and plopped down, wordlessly pointing Hank to the other chair.

Before he sat, he poured glasses of iced tea for each of them. Concern wrinkled his forehead as he sat the tea on the table, then took his seat across from her.

Lacey took a deep breath and plunged. "I've decided to practice law here, in West Monroe."

Hank twirled his tea glass, making a water ring on the table. The refrigerator hummed. The dishwasher sloshed. In the back of the house, the vacuum sucked up something that clattered and the boys giggled. Silent emotions chased across Hank's face, relief, gratitude, worry.

He took a sip of tea then carefully put the glass back into its wet circle. "I know how hard you've worked, how much your career means to you. Sacrificing all those years for Cody and me is more than I could ever ask of you."

Lacey covered Hank's hand with her own. "I would do anything for you and Cody. But I'm doing this for me. It's what I want, Hank."

He lifted her hand to his lips, a gesture of Old South gratitude and respect that made Lacey's southern heart skip a beat. "Thank you."

"It's my pleasure." Lacey leaned across the table, and Hank met her halfway. Gentle, warm, and oh, so tender, his mouth explored hers, nibbling on her bottom lip, tasting the corner of her mouth, making her hunger for more.

"Dad? Oh, Dad?" At first, Cody sounded a long distance away, a world away, then he sounded like he was right beneath her elbow. "Dad, I think the vacuum's broke."

With a sigh, Hank broke off the kiss.

Lacey opened her eyes to find that Cody *was* at her elbow. She blinked, trying to shake off her sweet, dreamy state and focus on what Cody was saying.

Through his glasses, Cody first studied Hank, then Lacey. Then he hollered down the hall, "B.J., you were right. And it was a big, sloppy one too."

"Told you so," B.J.'s cocky reply floated down the hallway.

"Dad, are you and Lacey getting married?"

Hank swallowed, his Adam's apple bobbing, then reached for Lacey's hand. "Yes, son, we are."

Cody cupped his hand to his mouth and yelled, "They are, Beej." Then in a normal tone, "If Lacey is B.J.'s sister and she's going to be my mother, does that make B.J. my uncle?"

The word *mother* blossomed in Lacey's heart until she thought her chest would burst with pride. Cody had said it so naturally, so acceptingly.

Hank cleared his throat. "I hadn't thought about it, but I guess so, son. Marrying Lacey will make B.J. your uncle."

"I don't have to do what he says just because I'm his nephew, do I?"

"No, son. You and B.J. will still be best friends just like you are now."

Cody studied a stain on the hem of his T-shirt, then pushed his glasses up on his nose and stared at Lacey, eye-to-eye. "You'll help with my math homework every night, right?"

"Every night, I promise."

"And I can make you cards on Mother's Day."

Her vision became too watery to see clearly. "I would be honored."

"And you'll sit next to Dad on the couch and watch TV with him when he's sad."

Lacey blinked back the tears and swallowed down the laughter that bubbled in her throat. "I'll even let him choose the channel sometimes."

"Then I'm glad you're marrying my dad and becoming my mom. This will be the family I've always wanted."

"Me too, Cody." Lacey opened up her arms, and Cody snuggled into her hug. She rubbed her cheek across his baby-fine hair, inhaling the warmth of small boy. "Me too."